"I do
sh

"Neither do I," he countered. "I've got a great idea. Let's not date together, starting with lunch. Do you like Chinese food? There's a nice restaurant a couple blocks from here."

"What about your head? Don't you have to rest?"

"My head's all better. Cured by your kiss," he explained before she could protest. "So what do you say? Let's grab a couple of egg rolls and have a little non-date conversation."

"I only get an hour."

"Cindy Marshall," he answered huskily, "if I weren't trying *very* hard to convince you of my sincerity, I'd have a shocking reply to that remark."

Caught up in the game, she tilted her head to one side and lowered her voice to a husky timbre. "And what would that be?"

"An hour is all the time I need, woman."

For the longest moment their gazes met and held. Something arced between them, something wild and sweet and primitive; emotions as old as time itself—passion, need, longing. She knew without a doubt that Brad Jordan wanted her...

Jan Mathews

Although she grew up on a farm in a small southern Illinois town and has lived in Chicago for over twenty-five years, Jan Mathews was born in Kentucky and still calls it home. She is a wife, mother, registered nurse, and writer—sometimes in that order. With a son who has a rock band and two other children who are involved in a variety of activities, she is always busy. If she could have one wish in life it would be forty-eight-hour days. She swears that her family, as well as every volunteer organization known to man, senses that she is a soft touch. She has been active in Scouting, athletic clubs, and in the PTA.

Jan's idea of heaven would be to spend a week in the wilderness—minus poison ivy—camping and backpacking. She would love to raft the Chattooga, see the Grand Canyon on horseback, and watch Monday Night Football without being interrupted.

Other Second Chance at Love books by
Jan Mathews

A FLAME TOO FIERCE #70
SEASON OF DESIRE #141
NO EASY SURRENDER #185
SLIGHTLY SCANDALOUS #226
THIEF OF HEARTS #273
SHADY LADY #306

Dear Reader:

What could be lovelier than a day in June? The next six SECOND CHANCE AT LOVE romances, of course! Jeanne Grant sets the tone by indirectly asking: Have you ever sympathized with the "other man" in romances? The guy who's nice, but ... well, he's just not the hero. Does he ever find the woman of his dreams? In *No More Mr. Nice Guy* (#340), Jeanne Grant shouts a resounding "Yes!" You see, Alan Smith is a wonderful guy, and Carroll's deeply in love with him. But sometimes she wishes he were just a little less ... well, less predictable, cautious, and controlled! And when Alan sets out to be dashing, macho, and reckless—watch out! With humor and insight, Jeanne once again creates a hero and heroine you'll simply adore ... and a one-of-a-kind love story that you'll savor and remember...

Next, Katherine Granger shows her admirable versatility in *A Place in the Sun* (#341), in which brooding, embittered Rush Mason is hired as groundskeeper by Libby Peterson, the ladylike owner of a Cape Cod inn. As Rush's powerful presence seems to shrink the lush acreage of Libby's seaside estate, their heated glances lead to sultry, sexually charged encounters that will make your own skin prickle! Slowly the tension builds ... the mystery about Rush deepens. Here's steamy reading for a warm, melting June afternoon.

What woman hasn't dreamed of meeting a dashingly handsome, thoroughly princely man who will sweep her off her feet and take her "away from all this"? In Sherryl Woods's latest romance, *A Prince Among Men* (#342), this secret desire is fulfilled for actress-mime Erin Matthews ... and the wisdom of "Be careful what you wish for because it might come true" takes on a whole new meaning! Mysterious Mark Townsend's majestic courtship of Erin will tickle your funny bone and tug on your heartstrings.

In an inspired move, Jan Mathews unites erotic dancer Cindy Marshall from her previous romance *Slightly Scandalous* (#226) and vice-squad cop Brad Jordan from *Shady Lady* (#306) to bring you another sassy, sexy romance—*Naughty and Nice* (#343). Though Cindy's now a respectable social worker, she can't forget that she once stripped for a living—and she *won't* get involved with a man as unsuitable as Brad Jordan! Easier said than done—because Brad storms all her defenses ... and in record time! No one creates tough guys like Jan Mathews ... and no one else could have written a romance as wacky and wonderful as *Naughty and Nice*.

Next, Linda Raye returns after a long hiatus with *All the Right Moves* (#344), in which two strong-willed characters find themselves on opposite sides of an issue ... and in constant disagreement over their romantic future! Basketball coach Ryan McFadden, who simply oozes sexuality, knows at once that referee Lauren Nickels is the woman for him. But Lauren's determined to remain aloof—no matter how roguish his charm or penetrating his insight! Still, Ryan sees that beneath her tough exterior there lies a woman's secret longing. With such great ingredients for romance, it's only a matter of executing all the right moves before love triumphs.

Kelly Adams has a special talent for capturing the spirit of America's heartland—both the richness of the land and the simple honesty of the people. In *Blue Skies, Golden Dreams* (#345), city slicker Sara Scott arrives on Joe Dancy's Iowa farm intending to rescue her sister from what she considers his con-artist clutches. But with lighthearted teasing, indomitable integrity, and stubborn persistence, Joe sets Sara to baking cookies and going fishing ... turning her into a country girl and stampeding her emotions in one fell swoop! In Joe's conquest of Sara, Kelly Adams conveys a breath-catching tenderness and a reaffirmation of good living that makes your heart sing.

Have a terrific June, everyone! Warm wishes,

Ellen Edwards

Ellen Edwards, Senior Editor
SECOND CHANCE AT LOVE
The Berkley Publishing Group
200 Madison Avenue
New York, NY 10016

SECOND CHANCE AT LOVE

JAN MATHEWS
NAUGHTY AND NICE

A SECOND CHANCE AT LOVE
BOOK

NAUGHTY AND NICE

Copyright © 1986 by Jan Milella

All rights reserved. No part of this publication may be reproduced or transmitted in any form or by any means, electronic or mechanical, including photocopy, recording, or any information storage and retrieval system, without permission in writing from the publisher.

Requests for permission to make copies of any part of the work should be mailed to: Permissions, Second Chance at Love, The Berkley Publishing Group, 200 Madison Avenue, New York, NY 10016.

First edition published June 1986

First printing

"Second Chance at Love" and the butterfly emblem are trademarks belonging to Jove Publications, Inc.

Printed in the United States of America

Second Chance at Love books are published by
The Berkley Publishing Group
200 Madison Avenue, New York, NY 10016

To all the members of the Chicago/North chapter of
the Romance Writers of America, with love.
With thanks for misshappen heroes,
for laughter, for love, and last, for your help.
And I promise never to do it again.
Also, to Virginia DeWeese, who suggested it,
and to all the Sindees in this world,
with love and thanks.

NAUGHTY AND NICE

CHAPTER
One

ALTHOUGH IT HAD been a long, tiring day, Cindy Marshall's mood was as bright and sunny as the July afternoon. After months of working with a particularly confused teenage girl at the Crisis Center, and getting nowhere, she had finally broken down barriers and made definite progress today. She wanted to celebrate. Success felt so good—almost as good as the sun on her shoulders as she stood waiting for the light to change on a busy downtown Chicago street.

"Isn't it a pity?" mumbled an elderly woman beside Cindy, *tsk*ing in disapproval. "Such a nice-looking young man, and not a soul cares. Hurry, hurry, hurry. A body could drop dead, and not a single person would stop to help."

Frowning, Cindy turned her attention to the woman, who had bent over to rummage through a wire-mesh trash can. Obviously a bag lady—one of the growing number of unfortunate people without homes—she was determinedly looking for something to add to her odd assortment of possessions.

"Now, when I was a girl, people helped each other," the woman prattled on. "When was the last time you saw someone help a blind person across the street?"

"Do you need help?" Cindy offered.

"Me?" the old lady snorted. "Don't be silly! I've lived in this city for years and can take care of myself. But that poor man..." She straightened up and gestured toward a tall man lounging carelessly against a lamppost a few feet away. "I've been standing on this corner for five minutes, and not a single soul has offered to help him. If I didn't have all these packages, I'd help him myself."

Poor man? Cindy doubted that observation. He was clad in loose-fitting slacks, a polo shirt, white deck shoes, and a jacket made from what looked like silk. But more than that, he was incredibly handsome: broad-shouldered, lean-hipped, blond, a real Adonis in the flesh. She must be blind to have missed him.

He seemed to be waiting for someone, or else he was lost in thought, for his hands were shoved deep in his pockets and he seemed to be gazing into space in a preoccupied manner. Instead of detracting from his appearance, his mirrored sunglasses gave him a certain mystique.

"Can't you see he's blind?" the bag lady declared, eagerly tossing an old magazine into a shopping bag from Saks Fifth Avenue. "And not a single person has come to his aid. Nobody cares. Why, we could all drop dead, and no one would care. Whoops, the light is green. Better hurry along, now, before we get run over. Chicago... I swear—"

As the crowd surged across the street, the old woman

followed, hauling her belongings and chatting away. Still watching the man at the lamppost, Cindy remained standing on the corner, letting people step around her.

Odd, he didn't look blind. He wasn't carrying a cane, and he didn't have a Seeing Eye dog. Yet he did seem to be staring off into space. And he wore those glasses.

"Look out, lady." A teenage boy shoved her sideways.

"Watch it!" someone else grumbled.

Trying to duck out of the way of passersby, Cindy glanced back at the man. Someone had bumped into him, too, but he managed to maintain his balance. If he *was* blind, a Chicago street corner wasn't a safe place for him to be stranded. In fact, a Chicago street corner wasn't a very safe place period.

Slowly she walked toward him. She was a social worker, wasn't she? And she could hardly ignore someone who needed help.

The man didn't move or look at her as she approached. A breeze from the lake ruffled his hair, lifting it slightly. Drawing closer, she could see her own reflection in his sunglasses. The wind had done more damage to her than it had to him. Convinced she looked a mess, she pushed a lock of long blond hair back from her face.

Now that she had decided to approach the man, what in the world would she say? *Can I help you cross the street?* seemed silly somehow. *Are you blind?* was worse. She cleared her throat. "Do you need help?"

She'd read somewhere that in blind people the unimpaired senses often developed beyond normal expectations. Perhaps the theory was true, because this man's hearing seemed to be phenomenal. Although she couldn't see his eyes behind the sunglasses, he appeared to be looking directly at her.

"What sort of help do you have in mind?" he said.

His voice was low and husky, yet smooth, like fine whiskey, and she felt strangely disconcerted by the boldness of his question. On top of that, he seemed to be gazing steadily at her. Could blind people stare?

"I wondered... I thought..." She cleared her throat again. Lord, she must sound really stupid. What if he wasn't blind? Would he think she was trying to pick him up?

Of course, nothing could be further from the truth. When it came to men, Cindy Marshall ran the other way.

Finally, not knowing what else to say, she blurted out, "I thought you might need help crossing the street." She gestured at the traffic zipping by. "There are a lot of cars."

"Cars?" he asked, turning toward the busy boulevard.

She felt compelled to explain. "Well, you're bli—I mean, you're wearing sunglasses."

"Sunglasses." He turned back to her. "Oh!" A slow grin lit up his face. "Yes, there are a lot of cars."

"They're going fast," she murmured, feeling hot and tingly all over as he seemed to focus his full attention on her. Again she had the uncomfortable feeling that he could see her. But she couldn't possibly be wrong about his being blind, could she? She frowned, undecided.

As if sensing her confusion, he said gravely, "Yes, the cars are going fast. I can hear them."

Sympathy won out over doubt. "I don't want you to get hurt."

"I appreciate that." His husky voice seemed to vibrate with poignancy. "Not many people are concerned about their fellow man these days."

"People tend to be callous," she agreed, hardly aware of her words. Unable to rid herself of the feeling that this blind stranger was staring down at her, she felt oddly mesmerized, and when he took her hand, a thrill of pleasure shivered through her.

"What's your name, honey?"

"Cindy Marshall."

Naughty and Nice

"Well, are you ready, Cindy Marshall?"

"Ready for what?"

"To cross the street." He grinned, a charming, lopsided smile. "Remember? Busy? Fast cars? I thought you were going to help me cross. You haven't changed your mind, have you?"

Cindy drew a deep breath to still her chaotic emotions. Good Lord, what was happening to her? She had to get hold of herself. She was a twenty-nine-year-old woman, not some sweet young thing who became tongue-tied whenever a handsome man glanced her way. "No, of course I haven't changed my mind," she said. "I'll be glad to help you."

"Good. Do you mind if I hold your hand?"

She did, but how could she say no to a blind man? "I don't mind."

"Good," he repeated, moving his callused thumb sensously across her palm and along her fingers.

Cindy glanced incredulously at the spot he was rubbing. What in the world was he trying to pull? The man certainly wasn't handicapped in all respects. Or did he think she had a message written in Braille on her palm?

"Excuse me," she said, trying to pull away.

"I'm sorry," he said quickly, tightening his hold on her. "I didn't mean to offend you. I just want to know what you feel like."

Offend wasn't an accurate description of what his touch had done to her. If she hadn't known he was blind, she'd have thought he was coming on to her. "You didn't offend me."

"Good."

Somehow, the way he said the word conveyed a wealth of innuendo. She was twenty-nine years old, she reminded herself again, and hardly naive. She'd been around the block more than once. She ought to know when a man was on the make. But this guy was blind, for goodness' sake! He couldn't possibly be flirting!

"How does my hand feel?" she asked.

"Very nice. Soft."

Frowning, Cindy reassessed him as he stared into space. If he was only pretending to be blind, he was doing an awfully good job of it. "What's your name?"

"Brad Jordan."

The name suited him. It was a rugged, strong name. "Which way are you going, Brad Jordan?"

He tilted his head toward her and leaned down as if to hear her better. "Whatever way you want. Where were you headed?"

"To the subway. I'm going home."

"And where's that?"

"I live in an apartment near Wrigley Field." They started across the street. "Watch the curb," she warned.

"Oh, yes. Thanks." He stepped down carefully, tightening his hold on her hand. "I'll bet you used to be a Girl Scout."

Cindy gave a half-laugh. "Me? Hardly."

With a past like hers? The woman who had founded that high-minded organization would turn over in her grave.

"Why not?" he probed softly.

"I don't know," she hedged, not wanting to think about her past. Although she had long ago accepted what she'd done as a teenager to survive on her own in a tough world, dealing with Nicole's problems today had made her aware of her lingering regrets. No Girl Scout would have done the things Cindy had done, or been so completely stripped of illusions at such a tender age. Then again, no Girl Scout was more deserving of a merit badge in survival.

"I could never sell cookies," she finally told Brad. "Were you a Boy Scout?"

"No, I couldn't sell cookies either."

Naughty and Nice

"Boy Scouts don't sell cookies."

"They don't?" he asked innocently.

He knew damned well they didn't. She smiled. Yes, Brad Jordan had quite a technique, particularly for someone who couldn't see. She wanted to ask how long he'd been blind and what had caused his disability, but she certainly didn't know him well enough to probe into his personal life, even if he *was* the sexiest man she'd ever met. She was helping him cross the street, nothing more.

At that very moment he tripped and fell hard against her.

"I'm sorry," she said, "I forgot to warn you about the other curb." She'd been too busy thinking about him. "Are you okay?"

"I'm fine, but..." He paused, as if undecided.

"Is something wrong?"

"It would be easier for me if we could walk closer together," he said, pulling her to his side and slinging an arm around her shoulders. "Like this."

Oh, right. As if she didn't know what he was up to.

Since it was a hot day, she was wearing a sundress that left her shoulders bare. He began caressing her arm in the same way he'd caressed her hand, moving his fingers sensuously over her skin. Obviously he'd been looking for an excuse to touch her.

In any other situation she would have pulled away and told him to get lost. But how could she object to a blind man's touch?

"Comfortable?" he asked.

"Yes, very comfortable," she murmured.

"My hand isn't bothering you, is it?"

"No," she said quickly, "not at all."

"You know," he went on, "pretty girls like you shouldn't be out on the street alone."

"Oh?" Unaccountably the compliment made her feel like one of the teenagers she counseled—all jittery and nervous. She shivered as he moved his hand across her shoulder. "Why not?" she asked.

"It's dangerous."

"Really?"

"Yes. In fact, it's highly perilous."

All at once the realization sank in. *Pretty!* How could he know she was pretty? The man was blind!

As her face flushed with anger and embarrassment, she jerked away from his grasp. "Wait a minute—"

"Oops," he said. "Sounds like I'm in trouble. Scam's up, huh?"

"How perceptive," she retorted dryly. "You'd better believe the scam's up! You can see!"

"Every luscious inch," he confirmed, his mirrored gaze traveling boldly up and down her body.

Cindy saw red. "Every *what?*" she nearly choked out.

"Uh-oh," he said, taking off his glasses and grinning unrepentantly at her. "Guess I goofed again. Don't you like compliments?" To her surprise he winked. His eyes were brown, she noticed, with gold flecks, and they seemed warm and friendly. Tiny crinkles creased the corners, suggesting that he laughed a lot, and for a moment the attraction between them seemed to go beyond the physical. "Listen, you can't blame a guy for looking," he went on. "You are luscious, you know."

Cindy's anger intensified. Friendly eyes, indeed! This man had played her for a fool! And he was ogling her again, his appreciative gaze traveling slowly over her, taking in the soft curve of her breasts, the slight roundness of her hips. She turned on her heel and began to stalk away.

"Hey, I'm sorry!" Quickly he grasped her hand. "Where are you going? Come back here."

Cindy glared at him, then at her wrist, where he was holding her. "Let go of me."

"Am I hurting you?"

"You have no right to touch me."

"True," he agreed, "and I'll let you go in a minute. But first tell me why you're so angry."

"Don't patronize me."

"Sweetheart, I'm not patronizing you."

"And don't call me *sweetheart*," she interrupted hotly.

"Cindy," he corrected, arching a single eyebrow at her. "Just for the record, I'm not patronizing you. I'm trying to continue our conversation. It seemed to me that we were getting along splendidly—until you got upset. If something I've done is bothering you, you'll have to spell it out."

"L-e-t m-e g-o," she complied. "In case you can't figure it out, that spells Let me go." She jerked her wrist from his grasp and started down the street again, but Brad caught up to her just as quickly as before.

"Okay," he said, falling into step beside her, "so I'm not blind. Is that what you're so angry about?" She didn't answer. Suddenly he began to limp. "Would you believe I'm lame?" He grinned. "Okay, I've got it. How about bad breath? We could have a Certs encounter."

"We won't have any further encounter." She paused, turning to him. "Mr. Jordan," she said, patiently drawing out the words, "I hate to break it to you, but despite evidence to the contrary, I am not stupid."

He appeared surprised at her annoyance. "I didn't mean to imply you were."

"Then what do you call what you're doing?"

"Making scintillating conversation?"

"Flippant is more like it. Or condescending." Why was she bothering to answer? She didn't owe the man anything.

"I'm trying to be entertaining."

"Well, you've failed, and I wish you wouldn't ridicule handicapped people. A physical impairment is very difficult to deal with."

"Did you think I was making light of a handicap?" he asked, turning serious. "Believe me, I didn't mean to. I just thought maybe you had a weakness for"—he paused, as though searching for the right word—"for people who need help. You know, some people take in stray animals. I thought maybe you had a weak spot for people with handicaps. I was hoping to capitalize on it."

"How sweet of you."

A lock of hair had fallen appealingly across his forehead, and he had jammed his hands into his pockets, making him look like a cross between a mischievous boy and a charming rake. "I'm a sweet guy."

"I'll bet."

"Oops, guess I goofed again," he said quickly. "Look, I'm sorry." To her surprise, his eyes reflected genuine regret. "I seem to be doing and saying everything wrong today. Let's start over." He put his sunglasses back on and held out his hand. "I'm Brad Jordan, and I'm glad to meet you."

But Cindy was still miffed. "You made a fool out of me. You pretended to be blind."

"I said I was sorry."

"You were wearing mirrored sunglasses," she went on in her defense. "You're *still* wearing mirrored sunglasses. I assumed—"

"You don't have to explain. I figured it out. When you stood in front of me and asked if I wanted help crossing the street, I thought you were pretty, and I wanted to get to know you. What's the matter with that? Don't you think you're overreacting a bit?"

Perhaps she *was* being overly sensitive. She certainly felt uncomfortable dealing with him as an admiring male. These days she felt uncomfortable dealing with *any* man who was attracted to her.

"Look," she said, "I'm not a pickup."

"A pickup?" he repeated, surprised. "You think I

thought you were a pickup, as in boy *picks up* girl—temporary chance encounter and all the connotations that go along with it?"

For a moment she thought he was going to point out that she had approached him, not the other way around, but instead he said, "Okay, respectability coming up." Before she could move, he gestured to a boy walking by. "Hey, kid—do me a favor, will ya? Say, 'Cindy Marshall, meet Brad Jordan.'"

The boy sized Brad up with a quick look. "You got to make it worth my while, mister."

"Of all the people on this damned street, I would connect with a ten-year-old hustler," Brad muttered, but he pulled a five dollar bill from his wallet and waved it in the air. "Go ahead."

"Cindy Marshall, meet Brad Jordan," the boy said.

Cindy couldn't stifle her grin as Brad handed over the money. "There," he said, turning to her. "All set."

"Anything else you want me to say, mister?" the boy interrupted, holding out his hand. "For a ten spot I'll say, 'Your place or mine?'"

"Get out of here, kid!"

Laughing, the boy ran off as Brad took a pretend swat at his backside.

"Little smart-mouth."

Cindy laughed, too, but she knew a formal introduction wasn't going to fix this problem. Only her leaving would. "Excuse me," she said. "It's been nice meeting you, but I have to get home."

Brad skipped ahead of her. "I'll take you there."

She hesitated. Did he really think he could pick her up one moment and escort her home the very next? The man moved awfully fast. She wondered what else he had in mind. "You'll take me there?" she repeated sarcastically.

She could tell from his quick grin that he got her gist.

"I already told you I was a sweet guy. I'm nice, too."

"Right."

"I swear." He held one hand up as if making a pledge. "And I already told you it's dangerous for a pretty girl to be out on the street alone."

"It's even more dangerous for a pretty girl to allow a stranger to escort her home."

"But we're not strangers," he pointed out, moving closer. "We've been introduced. And I'll have you know I'm not easy. I won't let you compromise me right away. You'll have to wait at least five minutes."

Cindy blinked in disbelief at his audacity. "Only five minutes? My, you must have trouble carting around your ego."

"Giant-sized, huh?"

"That's an understatement." She pushed around him, intending to walk away, but he reached out to grasp her arm.

"Hey, I was only teasing."

"I'm not," she said. "Look, it's illegal to accost women on the street. If you don't take your hands off of me, I'm going to yell for the police."

Although his smile broadened, he let her go, holding his hands in the air like a captured criminal. "Don't scream, now. Just hang on a second, okay?" In one quick movement he pulled a badge case from his breast pocket and flipped it open. "Chicago's Finest, at your service."

Cindy stopped dead in her tracks. She should have known. No wonder he'd been standing on the corner holding up a lamppost. He'd probably been on a stakeout, hoping to arrest someone. And he probably had a partner somewhere nearby. "So you're a cop," she said warily.

"Special vice task force."

"A vice-squad cop?" she repeated in disbelief, laughing. It sure did figure.

"Something wrong with that?"

Only if you counted all the times she'd been arrested by vice-squad cops in the past. "Not really."

"I promise not to run you in," he teased.

Of course he wasn't going to arrest her. She hadn't done anything wrong. Except for jaywalking once in a while, when she was too lazy to go to the nearest corner, she hadn't broken a single law in years. Yet at one time she'd have had reason to be wary of him. "I'll bet you're even carrying handcuffs."

"At the ready."

"Well, too bad I don't have time to try them on. It's been nice meeting you, Mr. Jordan."

"Brad," he corrected.

"Brad," she said, starting to back away. "Excuse me. I have to go home."

He followed. "I know. I'm ready whenever you are."

"Forget it."

"Why?"

"For starters, I'm sure you're supposed to be working on a case," she said, taking another step backwards. Lord, he was persistent.

"I'm working a minor bust. Nothing special."

"Isn't your partner waiting for you?"

They were still walking, she backwards, he forward. Brad kept smiling at her. "Nick won't even miss me."

A cop. She couldn't get over it! Of all people, she'd unwittingly gotten involved with a cop.

"Cindy, is something wrong?" Brad asked.

How would he react to the truth? *Hey, buddy, I used to be a stripper at Club Arnaud. When I was a teenager, I took drugs.* Probably he'd behave like every other man she'd told—with stunned disbelief, then revulsion. Maybe he'd be even more deeply shocked, since he was a cop.

"Wrong?" she asked. "Whatever could be wrong?"

"I don't know. You're acting strange."

She sure was. She hadn't behaved normally since the

moment they'd met. And he kept pressing her. She knew it was silly, but suddenly she felt frantic. She had to get away from him.

She glanced around, at that moment realizing that she was standing beside a subway entrance. Without pausing to think about it, she started down the stairs and into the station.

"What the hell?" Brad swore under his breath and called out, "Cindy!"

Since she used public transportation every day, Cindy always carried tokens in her purse. Quickly she found them, pushed one into the slot, slipped through the turnstile, and ran through the open doors of a train just before they closed. Taking a seat, she watched from the window as Brad Jordan ran into the station behind her.

As though by magic, his gaze found hers in the mass of homebound travelers. As the train started slowly forward, she couldn't tear her eyes from his.

Gradually the cars picked up speed and pulled into a dark tunnel. Cindy leaned back in her seat and took deep breaths, trying to calm her furiously pounding heart.

Brad Jordan had been right about one thing: She had overreacted to him. What was her problem? It wasn't like her to behave so ridiculously. Had she thought he could arrest her now for her long-ago indiscretions? Had she thought he could see beyond the woman she was today to the confused youngster she'd been then?

What would it matter if he could? She'd learned a long time ago that most cops weren't Officer Friendly. For a while, as a confused, defiant teenager rebelling against society, she'd been arrested so many times that a courtroom had begun to seem like home. But these days, in her job as a social worker, she dealt with the police department on a daily basis, and she no longer thought of law-enforcement officers as her natural enemies. So her reaction to Brad didn't make sense unless considered in terms of her past.

The lights illuminating the train flickered off and on, like a rapid blink. Cindy rested her head against the window and stared at the concrete tunnel zipping by. In less than half an hour she would arrive at her stop on the North Side. Soon the train would pass through downtown Chicago and travel aboveground for the rest of the journey home.

Cindy glanced up as a crowd surged onto the train at the next stop. Her eyes widened as she caught sight of a poster advertising a hot night spot called Club Arnaud.

The dancer on the colorful promotion was clad in a slinky sequined gown that dipped provocatively between her breasts. She was stripping off a pair of long gloves, her "naughty but nice" expression a classic. "For your entertainment pleasure," the ad read, "come meet Miss Betty Lu Wilkins, Chicago's own Gypsy Rose Lee, singing and dancing in an atmosphere of refined civility."

Refined civility. Tony Santini, the owner of Club Arnaud, had used that phrase many times in his advertisements, Cindy remembered ruefully. He liked the Gypsy Rose Lee ploy.

The supper club *was* exclusive. The prices on the menu were astronomical, and the people who attended were mostly affluent, the movers and shakers of the city. Once, years earlier, when Cindy worked there, she'd even danced for the mayor, going onstage as Freya the Viking warrior maiden, dressed in her golden chain mail, carrying her jewel-studded sword, and sporting a glittering coin in her navel.

She'd called herself "Sindee, with an S-i-n, which is what we could do together, baby," and at one time she would have had no qualms about coming on to Brad Jordan with that standard line. She'd been as brash and bold as a bright new day, taking delight in shocking people with her outrageous behavior. Yet she'd been torn up inside—as miserable and confused as the kids she now counseled.

Cindy stared at the poster, imagining herself in the picture instead of Betty Lu Wilkins. Like Betty Lu, she was blond, but her hair was longer, falling well below her shoulders. She was also taller, just shy of five feet seven, with blue eyes, not brown. Unconsciously she tugged at the top of her sundress. She'd filled out her costume better than Betty Lu did hers.

For a while, Cindy had been as much of a local celebrity as Betty Lu, although *notorious woman* might be a more accurate description. "I'll make a star out of you, babe," Tony had said, forgetting to mention that there was little glory and less fortune in being a star at Club Arnaud. Yet Cindy didn't harbor any animosity toward Tony Santini. Actually, she was grateful to him. Though he was a shrewd businessman above all, he'd given her a break when she'd most needed it—as a drug-addicted teenager with nowhere to go except down. She'd been fourteen the day she ran away from home and just under eighteen the night she'd stumbled onto Tony's doorstep and asked for a job.

It had been difficult to find work without any skills, particularly since she was just a kid... and hooked on speed.

Choices. Sometimes it seemed she'd made all the wrong ones. But coming to Chicago and finding Club Arnaud had changed her life for the better.

Tony had known that she was slightly underage. He'd known, too, that she took pills. He could have turned her out, but he hadn't; instead, he'd given her a job. And when she'd finally entered a drug rehabilitation clinic, he'd given her another break by promising she could come back to work at the club once she'd completed the treatment. She could stay as long as she needed to until she got her life in order. Although she had continued to work at Club Arnaud, doing the only thing she knew how to do—strip—she earned her high school diploma and enrolled in a college, eventually obtaining a master's degree. She'd long since stopped thinking about the runway and what she did on it. She had just been waiting for the day when she graduated and became a licensed social worker.

No, she wasn't upset with Tony. Four years ago, the night she graduated from college and retired from dancing, he'd hosted a party for her at the club. He'd even baked a cake.

She'd been twenty-five then, posied at the edge of a brand-new life. She was Cindy Marshall, social worker, no longer Sindee Marshall the stripper. No more late nights; no more hot lights. After seven years, no more bumping and grinding down a runway. That night she'd been so proud of her achievements; she was still proud of them. She'd survived tough times, earned her education the hard way, and fought to become a respectable, law-abiding citizen.

Cindy had reconciled herself with her past long ago, realizing that back then she'd done what was necessary to survive. But she no longer harbored any illusions about what other people thought of her after they learned her full story. Once, she had believed in love and marriage, and dreamed of them for herself, but bitter experience with men had taught her the foolishness of such illusions. Not one man she'd ever dated had been able to see beyond the things she'd done in the past to the person she was today.

You reap what you sow. An apt proverb. For most of her teenage years she had sown a wild crop. Was she paying for it now?

Purposely she concentrated on the head of the man in front of her, counting his gray hairs. She rarely thought about that time in her life, and she couldn't afford to dwell on it now. She was a different person. She had to forget and go on. It was just that she'd had so many reminders today—the encounter with Nicole, who was so much like herself at that age; the accidental meeting with Brad Jordan, a vice-squad cop; the poster of Betty Lu Wilkins. Then, too, there were some things she could never forget.

As a lonely teenager she'd tried to buy love with sex, and the inevitable disappointment of those liaisons had taken its toll. When she first started dancing at Club Arnaud, she hadn't dated at all. During her college days, she'd gone out with a few guys, but none of those relationships had worked out. Once the men learned how she earned her tuition, all they wanted was a quick tumble in bed. As time progressed, and she kept getting the same reaction from men, she gradually stopped seeing anyone at all—until last year when she met Peter.

Peter Ryan... tall, dark, handsome, morally upright, decent. She'd fallen head over heels in love with him. He'd seemed so different from the other men she'd known. But in truth he hadn't been different at all. She would never forget the look on his face the night she revealed the details of her past. At that moment, she'd become convinced that no matter what she did with her life, no man would ever want to marry her. She just wasn't a woman whom a respectable middle-class male could take home to Mother.

Her experience with Peter had been especially painful because she'd been so certain of his love. From the beginning she'd hoped that he would want to marry her. Not wanting to jeopardize her chances, she'd decided not to tell him about her past until they knew each other really well.

They had just made love. She'd given herself freely to him, and she'd wanted to be open and honest. But Peter had been horrified to learn of her past, unable to reconcile the woman he knew her to be with the shockingly different image she was now presenting to him.

Had it only been six months ago when he'd finally broken off completely from her? It seemed as if a lifetime had passed since then. The experience had confirmed for Cindy that, because of her past, no decent man would ever want to marry her.

She sighed and stood up as the train approached her stop. She'd started home in such a sunny mood. Then she'd met Brad Jordan, and everything had changed.

She hated to admit it, considering how he'd led her on, but he *was* charming. He was tall and handsome, too. And probably righteous, upright, moral.

A vice-squad cop.

As the train halted, she glanced at her reflection in the window and laughed. Men. She could sure pick them.

CHAPTER
Two

AS CINDY APPROACHED her apartment, the warm sun and a soft breeze off the lake restored her good mood. She walked down the street, swinging her purse and waving to people she knew. She lived several blocks from the elevated train, close to Lake Michigan in one of the old buildings in the Lakeview area. She happily put up with her third-floor apartment's banging pipes, squeaky floors, and unreliable heat and air-conditioning systems because she liked the neighborhood. It was an old, established community of people of all ages and ethnic backgrounds. Public transportation was easily accessible, and a major hospital was located nearby. Perhaps most important, winter or summer, it was only a short walk to the beaches and parks Cindy enjoyed so much.

She rounded the corner to her block and waved to Margie Saunders, a close friend from her Club Arnaud days, who was waiting on the stoop. "It's about time you got home!" Margie called. She was forty, a tall, buxom, and outspoken woman. She stood and twirled around, showing off her new dress. "What do you think?"

Margie had retired from dancing at the nightclub four years ago, at about the same time as Cindy, and now clerked in a store that sold slightly risqué garments. The dress she was wearing was fire-engine red, scooped low in front, and tight fitting around the hips. Margie's brassy red hair and buxom figure made the effect overwhelming.

"Nice," Cindy said.

"Really?" Margie frowned, glancing down at herself. "Don't you think it's too tight?"

"It is a little snug," Cindy agreed.

Margie grinned and smoothed the skirt over her hips. "Good. Then it's perfect."

Cindy laughed. It was just like Margie to like the dress because it was too tight. "Are you hungry?" Cindy asked as she pushed open the entryway door and started up the stairs to her apartment.

The two women frequently ate together. They both lived alone, but more than that, despite the eleven-year difference in their ages, they were close friends. When they'd worked together at Club Arnaud, Margie had been like a mother to her, particularly after Rebecca, her other mentor, had quit to get married.

"I didn't come over just to show you my dress," Margie said as she followed Cindy up the steps. "I'm starved. By the way, you're late. Where've you been?"

"Doing good deeds."

"Well, Saint Cindy, what's new about that? You do good deeds all day long."

Cindy laughed. Whenever she did anything good, Margie teased her about it. Margie's comment also made her remember the teenager she'd worked with that afternoon. "Sometimes I wonder if I actually accomplish anything good, although I did make some real progress with one of my cases today. Do you remember Nicole, the girl I told you about?"

"That kid who flipped out on speed last year and stole a car? I thought she'd been sent to reform school."

"No, I managed to get her placed in a foster home for a while. She's beginning to settle down now." Cindy couldn't reveal any more details of the case to her friend, but she had worked especially hard with this particular young woman, trying to keep her out of reform school. At Cindy's urging, Nicole had enrolled in a drug rehabilitation program and was beginning to confront the underlying causes of her problems. "If things keep going as well as they have been, she just might make it. I'm letting her go home for the weekend to visit her parents."

"I don't know how you put up with those teenagers. I couldn't stand it."

"You put up with me for years."

"You were different."

"Thanks." But Cindy wasn't certain she could consider Marge's comment a compliment.

At her landing, Cindy fished in her purse for her keys and unlocked the door to her apartment. As soon as she entered the room, her five cats came running to greet her. She scooped up Sam, the stray she'd adopted the previous December, thinking it was a boy. Sam had delivered Sparky, Jilly, Sasha, and Delilah six weeks later. She bent to stroke each kitten, cooing softly.

Margie, who hated cats, glanced down disdainfully as she sidestepped the felines and tossed her purse on the sofa. "Where do you want to go for dinner? I hear a nice place just opened over on Halsted Street."

"Why don't we eat here?" Cindy suggested. Back when she'd thought she might someday get married, Cindy had taken a gourmet cooking course. "Last night I tried out a new recipe."

But Margie felt the same way about gourmet food as she did about cats. She wrinkled her nose. "Did you fix it already?"

"All we have to do is heat it up."

"It." Repeating the word like a curse, Margie curled her lip in disgust. "I'm afraid to ask—"

"Goulash."

"Goul-what?"

Cindy laughed. "You'll like it."

"You said I'd like that pâté, too. It was liver."

"I promise you'll like this. It's a kind of stew."

"Did you make any dessert?"

"Pie."

Margie's expression brightened. "What kind?"

"No wonder your dress is tight," Cindy said. "You're eating too many desserts these days."

"Don't be a smart-ass. My dress is tight because I bought it tight. What kind of pie?"

"Apple spice."

"Whatever happened to plain old apple?" Margie grumbled. "I don't know what the hell apple spice is. And goul-hash for dinner?"

Cindy carried one of the cats into the kitchen. All the others followed, lining up in a row like little soldiers, meowing noisily, tails held high in the air. "You know what, Margie?" she said. "You're all bluff. You're wearing that tight red dress, yet if a man approached you, you'd run the other way."

"You're wrong there, kid," Margie retorted. "I may avoid the goody-goody types, but unlike *some* people I know, *I* like men."

Margie was always lamenting the fact that Cindy didn't date. "I like men," Cindy said.

"Could have fooled me."

Cindy shrugged. "Anyhow, you know very well what apple spice pie and goulash are." She opened cans of cat food and dumped them into two plastic dishes. "And how can you ignore these sweet little kittens?"

"I wish I *could* ignore the destructive little balls of fur."

"They're just playful," Cindy insisted. Although they were now almost as big as their mother, at six months of age the kittens were still playful. Unfortunately, very playful. Occasionally things got out of hand, but their destructiveness was accidental, and Cindy figured they'd eventually outgrow their mischievous ways.

"Oh, sure, they're playful all right," Margie said. "Look at this place. Your drapes are tied up because if you let them down, the cats will climb up them. Your furniture is covered so the cats can't chew the damned upholstery. All your plants, which took a long time to grow and desperately need light, are shoved in a closet." She gestured around the apartment, warming to her subject. "To top it all off, you can't keep the damned cats in the bathroom because they get in the toilet, and you can't keep them in the bedroom because they've figured out how to open the door and escape. You run around with a squirt bottle, zapping them with water and claiming you're training them."

"I *am* training them."

"Right," Margie said. "And I'm a nun."

It was useless to remark further on that particular topic. She and Margie would never agree on the subject of cats. "Do you want a salad with dinner?" Cindy asked.

"I didn't finish making my point," Margie insisted. "You've got all this love and energy. Why not lavish it on a man instead of wasting it on the stupid cats?"

They'd never agree on that subject either. What Margie didn't understand was that the cats couldn't hurt her and a man could. "Did you decide about the salad?" Cindy asked.

Margie sighed. "Julius, I suppose?"

"If by that you mean am I making a Caesar salad, yes." Cindy smiled sweetly. "And I'm so glad you like it. Shall we have croutons, too? Or should we diet?"

"Croutons, by all means." Margie pulled plates from a cabinet and started to set the table. "So tell me, aside from helping the kid, what other good deeds did you do today?"

"I helped a blind man cross the street." Cindy paused a moment, thinking of Brad Jordan. Vice-squad cops hadn't looked like him back when she'd been arrested. "Except he wasn't blind."

That got Margie's attention. She paused in setting the table. "What was he?"

"Nothing. Well, not *nothing*," Cindy corrected. "He was *something*—in fact he was gorgeous. But he could see perfectly well."

Margie sighed again and gestured toward the cats. All five of them had finished their dinner and were contentedly licking their paws. "You know, Cindy, I don't believe you. I swear you've got a soft spot for anything or anyone that needs help. So what happened when you helped this not-blind blind man across the street?"

Cindy laughed. "It's a long story."

"Don't want to talk about it?"

"Not really."

"But he was gorgeous?"

"Yes."

"How gorgeous?"

Cindy's soulful sigh conveyed impatience more than wistfulness. Sometimes Margie pushed her too hard. "He was a cross between yummy and wow; not at all blind, and it doesn't matter because I won't be seeing him again anyway."

"Why not"

"Why not what?"

Now Margie sighed impatiently. "Why won't you be seeing him again anyway?"

"He's not my type."

"Gorgeous isn't your type? Yummy and wow aren't your type? You know, Cindy, I think you've got a couple of screws loose. I suppose you're still pining away for old Peter Piper."

Margie hadn't liked Peter from the beginning. "His name is Peter Ryan," Cindy said.

"Piper's better. More descriptive. The guy reminded me of a pickle. His lips were always pursed up like a sourpuss." She demonstrated, then mocked, "'Peter Piper picked a peck of pickled peppers.' Hey! Remember when the men from the pickle-makers convention came to Club Arnaud? Now, *that* was a great bunch of guys." She smiled fondly. "There was one guy—what was his name? Fred? He used to stand on the table and shout and holler. I swear, he got so excited, I thought he was going to have a heart attack right there."

Cindy certainly did remember the pickle-makers. She didn't have any trouble recalling Fred, either. How could she forget? During her act she'd accidentally lost a pastie—one of the tiny slips of material that covered her nipples. Unfortunately, a couple members of the vice squad had been sitting in the audience, too. She and all the other dancers had been charged with indecent exposure and hauled into night court. Tony had been so mad that he'd refused to help her post bond.

Apparently Margie had a selective memory—for only the good times, not the bad ones. "They loved us," she went on. "All that cheering and clapping. Gosh, we were good. All of us... me, you, Rebecca. Cherry Wilder. Remember her? Last I heard, she'd moved to Arkansas and opened up a candy store."

"Arkansas is a long way from Club Arnaud, and selling candy's a long way from stripping," Cindy agreed.

"Crazy, huh? I can't imagine Cherry handing out sour balls to drippy-nosed little kids."

"I guess stranger things sometimes happen."

"I suppose." A faraway look came into Margie's eyes. "Gosh, I miss those days. You know," she said wistfully, "I was thinking... Maybe I'll make a comeback."

Cindy's eyes widened. "Margie, you're forty years old."

"So? I've still got all the right equipment." Margie laughed in her full-throated manner, then holding her hands over her head, she pushed her chest out and pretended to strut down a make-believe runway, singing, "*Ba*-da, *da*-da, *da*-dum. Baum! Baum! Baum!" With each *baum* she thrust her hips forward and around in the traditional bump and grind. "Say—" She stopped and gestured toward her nipples, moving her fingers in circles. "Can you still twirl your tassels in opposite directions?"

Good Lord, Cindy had forgotten about that. When she'd danced as Freya, the Viking warrior maiden, she'd sewn long gold tassels on her pasties. During her act she had twirled them around in circles.

"I remember you used to make them go up and down, too. 'Round and 'round and up and down. That was some talent, kid. I don't know any other dancer who can do it like you did."

"Neither do I."

"Well?"

"Well, what?"

"Can you still do it?"

"No."

"Have you tried?"

Cindy set the pan of goulash on the stove and flipped on a burner. "Margie, you may still be in shape, but I'm lucky if I can get my mascara on in the morning."

"I bet you could twirl them if you tried."

"Well, I'm not going to try."

"Why not?"

"Because."

Naughty and Nice

"Because why?"

Because it was silly. Because she was a different person now than she'd been then. "Margie, please, can't we talk about something else?"

"No. Why don't you want to try?"

"I don't know why!" Cindy snapped. She hated Margie's badgering. "I just don't want to!"

"Well, you don't have to bite my head off," Margie exclaimed, looking put out by Cindy's outburst. "All I did was ask a question."

Several questions, but Cindy didn't amend her friend's statement. She forced a bright smile. "Sorry. I didn't mean to snap at you. Look, would you mind coddling an egg for the salad? You know where I keep the pans."

"Looks like you're the one we need to coddle these days," Margie mumbled, still looking injured. "What the hell's eating at you?"

"Nothing. Look, I'm sorry. I just don't want to talk about the past. Can we change the subject?"

"Last year you used to love talking about the past. I'll bet we have old Peter Piper to thank for your change of heart. What exactly did he say to you to make you so down on yourself?"

Cindy closed the refrigerator door and turned to her friend. Despite Margie's show of concern, she didn't really understand. Yes, Cindy had accepted herself, made peace with her past, but there were times when she felt embarrassed about her former life—times like now when she remembered some of the outrageous things she'd done; times like this afternoon when she'd met Brad Jordan and yearned for a chance at a different life: a man to love, babies to raise, a home to build. Sometimes, no matter how good she felt about herself, she couldn't help regretting the past. And sometimes she desperately wished she could change it.

"I'm not down on myself," she answered finally. "I

just—You don't have a single regret, do you?"

"Regret?" Margie looked straight at her. "For what?"

"For stripping."

"Why? To punish myself? Honey, I took off my clothes, I didn't kill anyone. Cindy, you've got to learn to accept what you were."

"I *have* accepted what I was. It's just that sometimes I can't help wishing things had been different."

"I wish a lot of things could be different, too. Hell, I wish I were a skinny blonde. But look, kid, you can't change the past. And even if you could, what would that accomplish? You have to accept what you are today."

"I took drugs, Margie. Once I—" Cindy paused and drew a deep breath. "Once I even sold some speed to a friend."

"So? Your friend was hooked, too. You thought you were doing her a favor by selling her some of your stash. It wasn't like you were a real pusher, and anyhow, you got rehabilitated."

"That doesn't change what I did."

"Cindy, of all people you should know that guilt can be an awful trip. Don't judge yourself too harshly, love." Abruptly Margie bent and peered into a cabinet. "Now, where the hell is that pan?"

"You're the one who's trying to change the subject now."

"You bet I am. Philosophizing isn't my forte."

That was debatable. Certainly Margie always let her opinion be known. "Look farther back," Cindy said. "The pans are behind the skillets."

"Jeez." Margie grunted as she burrowed deeper into the cabinet. "This dress sure as hell wasn't made for performing domestic duties."

Cindy smiled as she turned from the sink. "Doesn't it come in a larger size?"

Margie leaned back on her heels, slightly out of breath, pot in hand. "Of course it comes in a larger size," she retorted, "but that's not the point. The point is, I've got the dress and I have to live with it."

Cindy knew Margie was referring to more than the dress. She might as well have said: Like it or not, you have to live with your past.

"I thought philosophizing wasn't your forte," Cindy said.

"Okay." Margie stood up, looking stern. "You asked if I had any regrets. Hell, no, I don't have any regrets. I was a stripper, and I loved every minute of it, and I don't give a damn what anybody thinks of me. Neither should you. If that's philosophizing, just call me Pluto."

"Plato," Cindy corrected.

"Whatever." Margie glanced down at the pan in her hand. "How the hell do I coddle an egg?"

Cindy gave her friend a quick, impulsive hug. "First you have to put an egg in the pan."

"Really? I would never have known." Abruptly Margie dropped her sarcasm. "I may be dumb, love, but I'm not stupid."

Cindy laughed, glad the tense moment was over. "Is there a difference?"

"There is. When you're dumb you don't realize what you're doing. When you're stupid, you know and do it anyhow." She pushed a kitten away with her foot. "Like taking in a stray cat and letting the damned thing have kittens. Scat!" she hissed, "before I make a fur coat out of you. Or like letting some nerd called Peter Piper make you ashamed of yourself," she added, picking up the thread of their previous conversation. "Now *that's* stupid."

For once Cindy couldn't argue. Turning away, she started to tear lettuce for the salad. They exchanged small talk while they finished fixing dinner, and later they watched the evening lineup of situation comedies on television.

When Margie finally went home, it was late. After

playing with the cats for a while, Cindy showered and picked out her clothes for the next day. The weather forecast was calling for more heat and humidity, so she pulled out a cool cotton skirt and a scoop-necked blouse in soft pink. She had a string of pearls and earrings that would go nicely with the outfit.

She pulled opened a drawer and rummaged around, only to discover her pasties while she searched for the necklace. Small, circular pieces of gold lamé with long tassels that caught the light, the pasties glinted up at her, reminding her of things best forgotten.

Why had she kept them? Four years ago they had reminded her of the tassels on her graduation cap and inspired her to keep plugging away on her degree. Today they just looked ridiculous.

Picking them up, she turned them over in her hand, allowing the silky tassels to sift through her fingers. She hesitated a moment, wondering if she could still twirl them in different directions. Then she laughed and tossed them back into the drawer. Even if she could twirl the darned things, what would it prove? That she was still a talented stripper? Just what she wanted to forget.

Cindy was busy all the next morning and didn't have time to dwell on her problems.

She started the day late, since her alarm didn't go off on time, and she had to rush to get to work by nine. Then, typically, she seemed to be behind schedule the entire morning. It was a frantic morning, too.

The clinic where she worked was one of the best in the city, particularly when it came to meeting the needs of teenagers. Located downtown in the Loop, the Crisis Center was run by the county. Despite its prestigious address, there was nothing imposing about the place. It was housed on the first floor of one of the older buildings, in what looked like a storefront. Several smaller rooms branched off of a large reception area. Rock music played over a stereo system, and the decor was bright and bold, designed to appeal to teenagers, in the hope that they'd feel comfortable and be able to interact with the social workers. Double glass doors led to a medical clinic where doctors and nurses were available around the clock. Upstairs, a few bedrooms accommodated those kids without places to sleep for the night.

When Cindy's last case of the morning left—a teenage boy with a long history of petty crime who had just confessed to stealing a record from a store, just for the hell of it—Cindy leaned back in her chair, glad it was almost lunchtime. The pile of papers on her desk was daunting, but filing them could wait. First she needed a cup of coffee.

She reached for her purse and pulled out her sunglasses. As the weatherman had promised, the day was bright and sunny. She'd grab a sandwich from the café down the block and go for a walk along the lakefront. Perhaps the sand and the breeze would help her relax.

As she glanced down at the sunglasses in her hand, an image of Brad Jordan came to her mind's eye—a tall, handsome mirage grinning down at her, his hands shoved nonchalantly into his trousers pockets. What would it be like to be loved by a man like that? To marry him? She could so easily imagine the Victorian house with a white picket fence, wild pink roses growing in the back yard. Roses with soft, pale buds. The two of them sitting in a swing on the front porch, watching their children play on the green, manicured lawn...

Forget it, Cindy, an inner voice advised. *You don't have a chance with a man like Brad Jordan.*

She sighed. How true. A former stripper and a vice-squad cop—what a ridiculous combination! But he was so handsome, and despite his teasing, she had sensed his genuine interest in her.

Enough!

Sighing again, she stood and slung the strap of her purse over her shoulder, then started to leave—but she halted abruptly in surprise when she nearly ran into Brad Jordan himself, standing in her doorway, grinning at her!

He was wearing the same aviator sunglasses and clothing similar to the day before—loose slacks and a jacket—and despite the wide white bandage around his head, he looked as tall and tan and handsome as ever. Sweeping off his glasses, he leaned against the door frame and shoved his hands deep in his pockets. "Good morning."

His voice was as smooth and husky as before. Cindy wanted to melt. She stood mute for several minutes, staring at him in disbelief. He must be an apparition, a vision conjured up by wishful thinking. He couldn't be real! But how many ghosts appeared with white bandages around their foreheads?

How had he hurt himself?

Finally she murmured, "Hi."

"Fancy meeting you here. Some coincidence, huh?"

"Yes, it is."

He nodded at her desk. "Busy day?"

"Yes."

"Looks it."

Slowly Cindy glanced back at her desk as if to reassure herself that she was, indeed, at the Crisis Center in downtown Chicago and not dreaming. She turned to him again, puzzled by his presence and by the bandage on his head. "A nurse should be on duty next door."

"I know, I've already seen her."

"How did you hurt yourself?"

"I hit my head on my car door."

She grimaced. "That's too bad." Trying to assume a professional demeanor, she added, "What can I do for you?"

"Plenty," he said, his grin broadening, "but I'll let it

pass for now. Aren't you going to ask me how I'm feeling? I had to pay five bucks for this bandage—it's called a Kling. The nurse... Molly?... assured me it was authentic."

"Which is authentic," Cindy asked seriously, even more confused, "the head injury or the bandage?"

"I'll let that pass, too. Ask me how I'm feeling."

"How are you feeling?"

"Terrible. My head hurts."

"Oh."

"Don't you feel sorry for me?"

Cindy licked her lips uncertainly. If he was truly hurt, she would feel sorry for him, but after yesterday, she suspected he was spoofing her. "Maybe. What are you doing here?"

"I brought you a case. Or rather, I brought one of your colleagues a case." He nodded toward the other room. "A kid from Juvenile."

"That was considerate of you." It was also unusual. Cindy wasn't certain, but because he worked in plain-clothes, she suspected Brad Jordan was a senior detective. Cops at that rank, she knew, very seldom transported juveniles.

"I'm a considerate guy."

"Yesterday you told me you were sweet," she said.

"I'm that, too. May I sit down? Molly said people with head injuries should relax." Without waiting for her answer, he entered the office and slouched in a chair, stretching his legs out comfortably in front of him. Watching him, Cindy felt her heart do weird flips and somersaults. Weakly, she sank down into her chair. "Do you have a car?" he asked.

"No, I don't. Why?"

"If you'd ever hit your head on a car door, you'd know how badly mine hurts."

"I take the elevated to work."

"I know, but what about when you visit your relatives out in the suburbs?"

"I don't have any relatives."

"No brothers? Sisters? Mom or dad?"

"No." She didn't know what else to say. She could hardly blurt out that her mother was a drunk and her father worse and that she'd run away from home the night her father, in a drunken rage, had beaten her. Her usual lie—that they were dead—suddenly seemed too obvious a fabrication.

"Grandparents?" he asked.

"No," she answered quietly.

"No significant others at all?"

"No, none." But she smiled at his use of the psychological jargon. "I have friends, of course."

"I hope so. People shouldn't be alone in this world, especially pretty girls like you."

Even his style was smooth. Pretty girls, indeed! "Does your head really hurt?"

"If it did, would you feel sorry for me?"

"Yes."

"Good."

Never in her life would she have believed that a single syllable could sound so sexy. Or that a single man could have so much sex appeal. Brad Jordan exuded male sensuality—from his bandaged head right down to his well-soled toes.

"I need somebody to feel sorry for me," he went on. He stood up and walked to her desk, picking up a marble paperweight and lightly caressing it as he spoke. "But a kiss would make it better."

"What?" She'd been lost in her own thoughts—thoughts of his voice mesmerizing her, thoughts of his hands caressing her.

Before she could react, he leaned over her, his lips coming close. "I said, a kiss would make my head feel better. In fact"—the words were a mere whisper between them—"a kiss might even cure it."

His mouth met hers. Soft. Feathery. Brushing light strokes across her lips, he was a master artist putting the last, loving touches on a canvas of soft pinks and violets.

Like pale rosebuds. Which reminded her of a picket fence and a wide porch with a swing.

The kiss ended all too soon, and with it, Cindy's vision. She blinked as Brad drew back slightly.

"Are you ready to go?" he asked huskily.

Sure am, she wanted to say. *For whatever you want to do.*

Although the kiss had been brief, she felt as if an avalanche had bowled her over. She had to get herself together! She cleared her throat and set up straighter in the chair. "Ready to go where?"

"To lunch."

He was grinning again, one hand on her desk, the other on the back of her chair. She could feel his nearness, an awareness of him like electricity in the room. "I can't go to lunch."

"Why not?"

He'd asked a simple question, but she was finding it hard to think. "It's not time for lunch."

"Why would Molly lie to me about that?"

Cindy was having difficulty following his conversation. She frowned. "What are you talking about?"

He gestured toward the door. "Molly, the nurse at the medical clinic. When I called earlier, she told me you always go to lunch at noon." He glanced at his watch. "It's ten past now."

Cindy chewed her bottom lip for a moment, searching for an excuse. She couldn't go to lunch with him. The man was devastating to her senses.

She gestured at the clutter on her desk. "I do usually go at noon," she said, "but I'm too busy today."

Brad inclined his head toward her purse, the strap of which was still slung over her shoulder. "Do you always protect your personal belongings by keeping them so close to you? Must be tough to work that way."

She was caught in a web of her own making. "No," she admitted.

"You were going to lunch, right?"

She might as well admit the truth. "Right."

"And you don't want to go with me," he added. "You're trying to think of an excuse."

She nodded. "Yes."

"Do you have any idea how badly you've damaged my ego? It may be giant-sized, but you've just put a chink in it as big as a mortar shell. If you keep on, I'll be mortally wounded."

Do you have any idea how you've affected me? she wanted to say. Instead she murmured, "I'm sorry."

"So am I. Tell me, Cindy Marshall, why are you afraid of me? What have I done to frighten you?"

He'd done everything to frighten her—and yet he'd done nothing. What a contradiction. How could she explain that?

"It's not you, exactly," she said. She tried to back away, but the way he held on to her chair made moving from him an impossibility. She was trapped. She had to breathe his scent, a tantalizing blend of warm male flesh and spicy after shave, but worse, she had to feel his nearness.

"What is it, exactly?"

She couldn't tell him the truth. *I'm a former stripper* would sound as blunt today as it would have yesterday. "I don't date," she said.

"Neither do I," he countered. "I've got a great idea. Let's not date together, starting with lunch. Do you like Chinese food? There's a nice restaurant a couple of blocks from here."

Persistent didn't begin to describe Brad Jordan. She didn't believe for a moment that he didn't date. Women probably fell at his feet in droves. "Don't you have to be at work?"

"I'm a vice-squad cop, remember?" he answered. "I work at night—when the criminals work. It's a nice, lazy life."

She didn't believe that either. "What about your head? Don't you have to rest?"

"My head's all better." Quickly he unwrapped the bandage and tucked it into a back pocket. As he grabbed her hand, she saw no sign of an injury. "Cured by your kiss," he explained before she could protest. "So what do you say? Let's grab a couple of egg rolls, some fried rice, have a little non-date conversation." Absently, or so it seemed, he traced tiny circles in her palm with one finger. "We could also go for a walk along the beach."

Despite her reluctance, Cindy smiled. There was no denying that the man was charming. "I only get an hour," she said.

"Cindy Marshall," he answered huskily, "if I weren't trying *very* hard to convince you of my sincerity, I'd have a shocking reply to that remark."

Caught up in the game, she tilted her head to one side and lowered her voice to a husky timbre. "And what would that be?"

"An hour is all the time I need, woman," he answered.

For the longest moment their gazes met and held. Something arced between them, something wild and sweet and primitive; emotions as old as time itself—passion, need, longing. She knew without a doubt that Brad Jordan wanted her. But suddenly his expression turned serious. "Aren't you hungry? I sure am."

She laughed aloud. She had to admit he was resourceful. If one tactic didn't work, he tried another. "Yes, I am hungry."

"Then let's go. No more excuses. We can't let this second coincidental meeting go uncelebrated. Don't forget that old saying."

"What old saying?"

"If you meet somebody by coincidence more than once, you're indebted to him for life."

"That's not an old saying. You made that up."

"Caught again." Abruptly he pulled her to her feet. "Oh, one other thing." He paused. "You won't try to run away from me again, will you?" As the intensity of his gaze and the warmth of his firm grip on her hand seeped into her awareness, Cindy felt her resolve melting away. He was not only inventive, he was strong and forceful, too. All in all, Brad Jordan possessed a magic combination of qualities that she found impossible to resist.

And suddenly she didn't want to resist him. She wanted to be with him, wanted to pretend—if only for a short while—that a man like Brad Jordan could want someone like her. She needed to believe in her flight of fancy—those soft colors and that picket fence.

"No, I won't run away," she promised.

She walked beside him to the door. Anyway, she told herself as he took her arm and led her out of the building, what real harm could come from sharing egg rolls and fried rice? It wasn't as if they were making a lifetime commitment to each other. A little non-date conversation, a walk along the lakeshore if there was time. That would be pleasant.

And after today, she would never see him again.

CHAPTER
Three

THEY WALKED THE two blocks to the restaurant. Being so close beside Brad, Cindy felt even more nervous. Her anxiety level only increased when they entered the restaurant, which was darker and more intimate than she would have liked. But it was too late to object. She did have only an hour for lunch, and she'd already wasted a quarter of it trying to get out of going with Brad, whose hand at the small of her back guided her to their booth. The warmth of his touch burned her flesh through the thin fabric of her dress.

Just then, a tall, dark man paused beside her. "Say! Don't I know you from somewhere?"

Cindy stiffened. "No, I don't think so."

"I'm sure I know you," the man insisted, moving closer. "I never forget a face." He grinned as his glance encompassed more than her profile. "Or a body."

"Pardon me?" Cindy said coldly.

"Hey, no offense. You're a beautiful woman," he went on, studying her intently. "I know I've seen you somewhere before. Your face... do you work near here?"

She felt herself turn pale. Why now? Why today? Obviously the man had recognized her from Club Arnaud. All she needed was someone reminding her of her past in the middle of a crowded restaurant.

"I remember now," the man went on, stepping closer to her. "You're—"

"Excuse me, buddy." Brad's words were a low threat. He put his hand on the man's shoulder. "The lady's got an escort."

The man shrugged. "Sorry, pal. I didn't mean to infringe."

Brad put his arm around her waist and pulled her close. "Let's go," he said.

Although the restaurant was filled to capacity with a lunchtime crowd, the tall booths and strategically placed plants essentially separated the groups of patrons from one another. The decor was colorful and ornate; intricately carved replicas of dragons and plum blossoms, fragile and lovely, hung from the ceiling, as did gaily colored lanterns with long gold tassels—alarmingly similar to the ones tucked away in Cindy's dresser drawer. She looked away, embarrassed. When they reached their table, she sank down into the booth, grateful for the privacy. A small lantern illuminated the booth with a soft glow, and a kite in the shape of a dragon adorned the wall.

"You never answered my question," Brad said after the waiter had set a pot of tea on the table. "Do you like Chinese food?"

"I adore it," Cindy answered. "I could eat egg rolls twenty-four hours a day."

"Good, I like Chinese food, too."

"Do you eat out a lot?" she asked, imagining he did in his line of work.

"Yes, but usually fast food. That's about all a cop has time for." He shrugged. "Consequently, most of us end up with ulcers. A real meal is a treat."

"Don't you cook?"

"Not ordinarily. I don't see the sense in it for one person. But give me a charcoal grill and some hamburgers and two or three guests, and I rival any outdoor chef. Do you like barbecued food?"

"I like spicy food," she said. "I lived in Texas for a while and developed a taste for Mexican dishes."

"Sounds like we have something else in common. I like Mexican food, too." He held up the teapot. "Tea?"

"Please." She pushed her cup toward him.

Now what? She wished the waiter would come. The sooner they ordered, the sooner she could get away from Brad Jordan. Letting him take her to lunch had been a mistake. The restaurant was too darned dark, and even across the table he was too darned close. And he was smiling at her.

Instead of the diversion Cindy hoped for, just then, two social workers from the clinic approached their table. Darlene was tall and darkly attractive. Linda was a voluptuous blonde. "Well, hi, Cindy!" Darlene exclaimed, sounding as though they were long-lost friends who hadn't seen each other in years instead of minutes. "What are you doing here?"

"Eating lunch." Cindy wanted to laugh as Darlene's gaze roamed freely over Brad. The two women's interest was so obvious! Yet, Cindy had to admit, he *was* irresistibly attractive.

"Us, too." Linda gave Cindy a questioning glance that said: Aren't you going to introduce us? "Did you have a busy morning?"

"Yes, I did." Amused, Cindy wondered just how far

her friends would go. She smiled at Brad, who gave her a silent, questioning glance.

Darlene wasn't as subtle. She kicked Cindy under the table. "You work too hard, hon. You should take a couple days off."

"I have vacation time coming up soon."

Finally Linda grew tired of waiting. She smiled shyly at Brad. "Hi, there."

He smiled back. "Hi."

Cindy gave up her pretense. "Oh, didn't I introduce you? I'm sorry. Darlene, Linda, meet Brad Jordan."

"It's nice to meet you," Darlene drawled.

"Yes," Linda added, "very nice."

Cindy sighed as the two women practically fell over themselves trying to shake his hand. The man wasn't *that* attractive. She glanced at him again, then back at the two women. On the other hand, he had an awfully nice smile.

"Nice to meet you both," Brad answered. "Are you alone?" For a moment Cindy thought he was going to invite them to sit down, but he stood and gestured toward a waiter. "Excuse me, but these two pretty ladies need a table."

"We already have a table," Linda said, disappointment threading her tone. Obviously she'd hoped he would invite her to sit with him.

Brad smiled at her, a characteristically charming half-grin. "Oh, well, have a pleasant lunch."

"We will." Darlene rolled her eyes at Cindy as if to say, Lucky stiff. "Bye."

"I'm sorry," Cindy said after her co-workers had left, and Brad had sat back down. At least the two women had managed to break the ice. Cindy didn't feel half as uncomfortable with him now as she had before.

"Don't worry about it. I enjoyed every moment."

She'd just bet he had, but before she could say anything more, the waiter came to take their order. "Do you live in the city?" she asked abruptly when the formally attired man had left.

"I have a small apartment on the near North Side."

"Your typical everyday bachelor pad?" She'd always suspected that men who looked like Brad Jordan maintained regular dens of iniquity with mirrors, water beds, satin sheets, piped-in stereo music, and women by the thousands. Linda and Darlene would certainly have volunteered to complete the decor.

"That depends on what you mean by typical and everyday," he answered. "There are socks on the floor, and I keep forgetting to do the dishes. It's pretty small, just a studio. How about you? Do you have a big place?"

"I have three rooms. It's large enough, particularly when I have to clean it."

"That's why I like closets," he said.

She frowned. "I don't understand."

"You can throw things in them. Makes cleaning up a cinch."

She laughed. "And I thought you were hiding some deep dark secret. You know, the proverbial skeleton in the closet?"

"I have a couple of those, too," he said. "In fact, would it surprise you if I told you I have a police record?"

"You?" She certainly *was* surprised. "But you're a cop."

"So?"

"Can someone with a record become a policeman?"

"You're looking at living proof. Of course, your everyday murderer, or anyone who's committed a felony, wouldn't be accepted to the academy."

"How did you break the law? Park illegally?"

"Hey! I'll have you know I committed some real live misdemeanors in my time."

She glanced at him in disbelief. "Sure."

"It's true," he insisted. "When I was a kid I got into some trouble. Right here in Chicago. Close by, in fact."

If he really had a record, it was probably for making an improper turn or something equally as innocuous. Cindy frowned. "And here I thought you were a suburbanite."

"I'm that, too, I guess. I was raised in the city, but my folks moved to the suburbs when I started high school. When I decided to join the police force, I moved back. Chicago cops are required to live in the city."

The mention of a police record surprised Cindy and piqued her curiosity. "What made you decide to become a policeman?"

"The real reason or the proclaimed reason?"

"They aren't one and the same?"

"Not at all. The real reason I became a cop is because we get to carry guns, speed around the city in fast cars, work nights, look macho, have pretty women approach us on street corners." He grinned, reminding her that she'd approached him on a street corner. "All in the name of upholding the law."

Cindy was certain his job entailed a little more effort that he was suggesting, but she couldn't help smiling. He *was* macho, and she'd be willing to bet he did love speeding around the city in fast cars. He probably enjoyed anything that was dangerous. "And the proclaimed reason?" she asked.

"To please my mother. She got tired of bailing me out of jail. By the time I was sixteen I had a sizable collection of mag-wheels." At Cindy's blank look he explained, "You know, those fancy rims on car wheels."

She didn't believe him for a single moment. He probably had all sorts of good reasons for being a policeman, and she'd bet the only mag-wheels he had were the ones on his own car. No doubt he felt uncomfortable talking about himself and was trying to impress her with his macho facade. "What did you do with them?"

"I sold them. I made a profit, too." He grinned at the eyebrow she arched in skepticism. "At least I was enterprising."

She shook her head. "I suppose it's important to be enterprising."

"It is," he said seriously. "Very important."

For once Cindy believed him. Where she was concerned, he'd certainly demonstrated boldness—coming to the clinic, maneuvering her into going to lunch with him. Yet in spite of his teasing banter, Brad Jordan struck her as being very serious about his job. The entire time they'd been in the restaurant he'd been alert to everything going on around them. She couldn't see his gun, but she knew he carried one, for occasionally when his jacket opened, she caught a glimpse of his shoulder holster.

"Does your mother still live in the suburbs?" she asked.

"Yes, Downers Grove. My sister and brother live out in the boonies, too. I'm the only city dweller."

"You make it sound as if we're all cave dwellers."

"It's a jungle out there, babe."

It certainly was a jungle, and if Cindy wasn't more careful, she'd end up being preyed upon. She felt much too comfortable in Brad's presence. Their meal came, and they began to eat while they talked. She wasn't certain just when she started to relax and enjoy the conversation with Brad, but suddenly she realized she wasn't at all anxious. The man still intimidated her sexually, particularly when his hand brushed against hers or when his pant leg met her bare calves under the table, but otherwise he no longer seemed a threat.

"Do you have a big family?" she asked.

"Not really. There are only three of us—my brother, my sister, and myself, as well as my mother and stepfather. I'll take you to meet them sometime. If you like the suburbs, you'll love Downers Grove."

"What makes you think I like the suburbs?"

"There's lots of lawn—"

"—to mow," she interrupted.

"Wide open spaces—"

"—for the wind to roar through."

"A big driveway—"

"—to sweep."

"Trees—"

"—that shed leaves you have to rake up."

He laughed. "I can't believe I was wrong about you. For some reason I thought you'd like the suburbs."

The fact was, she did like the suburbs, but how had he possibly guessed that? "You weren't wrong about me," she admitted. "One day I would like to live in a small town." With a man who loved her and children to care for, she silently added.

"Anyplace special?" Brad asked.

Cindy shifted uncomfortably. In a moment she'd be describing her Victorian dream house with its pink rosebushes, picket fence, and the swing on the front porch. "No, nowhere special," she said.

He didn't seem to notice her evasion. "So, tell me, what do you do at the Crisis Center? Besides keep your purse close by, that is."

She scowled at him in mock rebuke for teasing her. "Lots of things. I find foster homes for kids, refer them to specialized agencies, counsel families and individuals of all ages." She shrugged. "Mostly, though, I work with teenagers."

"Do you enjoy that?"

"Sometimes I feel like a cross between the Good Witch of the North and a gestapo agent, but yes, in general I like my work."

"A lot of people don't like kids that age," he answered. "I think teenagers are special people. Hell, I was a teenager myself once, and I sure made my share of mistakes."

So had she.

But Cindy was warming to the subject and not about to be put off by her memories. She liked talking about kids.

"It's a difficult time of life," she agreed. "Teenagers face so many conflicting emotions, so many decisions, and it doesn't help that they're experiencing extreme hormonal shifts and surges."

"Do you mean that in addition to everything else, they have to cope with their sexual awakening?" he paraphrased.

She'd been thinking more along the lines of acne and growth spurts, but she nodded. "A person's sexual awakening can be at least as traumatic as pimples."

He laughed. "In a police magazine, I once read about a theory that some criminals commit crimes because of hormonal imbalances."

"That's hard to believe."

"It is an odd theory," he conceded. "But I wouldn't be surprised if it turns out to be true. Certainly what I see on the streets every night substantiates it."

She gathered he wasn't referring to anything as simple as jaywalking. Despite her past and the things she'd seen and done, as a big city detective, he'd probably experienced things that she could only imagine. "Is this your district?" she asked.

"No. As a detective on the special vice task force, I range pretty much citywide."

"Sounds exciting."

There was a brief silence. Then Brad said, "So tell me about your friends."

"My friends?"

"Yes." He poured more tea. "You said you have some friends, but no family."

She could hardly tell him about Margie. What would she say? *I have a friend who used to strip, just as I did.*

You'd like her. She wears flashy red clothes and speaks her mind. "Oh, my friends aren't all that unusual."

"Any of them live near you?"

Now she was in trouble. "Margie does."

"So tell me about her. What does she do for a living?"

Why was he pursuing this line of conversation? Cindy put down her napkin and pretended to search in her purse for something. "She's a sales clerk."

"Do you live alone?"

And if she did, how convenient for a man on the make. She glanced up sharply at him and realized he wasn't leading her on. He was just interested in her. She smiled. "Yes, I do live alone. Well, except for my cats."

"Cats?" He smiled, too.

"I took in a stray last winter that I mistakenly named Sam. She turned out to be a pregnant female. I didn't have the heart to give the kittens away."

"So you're stuck with them."

"Yes."

"I was right, you know."

"What about?"

"About you being a soft touch. You take in strays in addition to helping the handicapped."

"I'll never live that down, will I?"

"No. Tell me, what other good deeds do you do?"

Saint Cindy, Margie called her. She shrugged. "Not much, I guess. I work with kids. I volunteer at an old folks home every week. Sometimes I serve as a block captain for the heart disease fund-raising drive. Why?"

"No special reason. Just getting to know you. Do you know how to dance?"

The man was the strangest conversationalist she'd ever encountered. What did dancing have to do with doing good deeds? "Yes," she said, unwillingly reminded of the seven years she'd supported herself as an exotic dancer. "I know a few steps."

"Could you teach me?"

"You don't know how to dance?" They had finished eating, and Cindy was sipping tea. As he spoke, she paused and held the cup to her lips.

"I never learned. As a kid I was too busy stealing hubcaps, and as an adult I was too busy being a cop. But we're having a policemen's ball next month, and I'd like to go. I thought maybe you'd go with me."

Cindy felt as if her stomach was falling to her toes. She couldn't got to a policemen's ball. It was unthinkable. "Brad, I—"

"Don't say no yet," he interrupted. "You'll wound my ego again. Cindy, don't you like me?"

How could she explain what she felt for him? "I like you a lot," she said softly, "but—"

"Good. By the way, it's a formal dance. I have to wear a tuxedo. I'm sure you must have a gown."

Just then the waiter brought their bill and two fortune cookies. Cindy sighed, but before she could explain her reluctance to be with him, Brad broke open a cookie and pulled out the small slip of paper tucked inside.

"Do you believe in fortunes? I do. Listen, mine says, 'In the very near future you will become involved with a gorgeous blue-eyed blonde named Cindy.'"

She smiled and reached for the paper. "I'll just bet it says that."

Sure enough, the words jumped out at her, exactly as he'd read them. Brad indicated the other cookie on the plate. "What does yours say?"

Though she knew she ought to eat the cookie and ignore the fortune—or perhaps the other way around— Cindy pulled out her fortune without reading it and handed it to him.

"Hmmm," he said, arching his eyebrows at her and pretending to be surprised. "'Tall, handsome man across table called Bradley Jordan is perfect catch for girl named

Cindy. She should honor and obey him.'"

"Custom-made fortune cookies? Just who do you know here?" she exclaimed, laughing.

"Nobody," Brad insisted, shaking his head. "Not a soul. I've never been here before in my life."

"Right," she said dryly. "Your full name is Bradley?"

"Yes, isn't it awful?"

"I think it's a nice name."

"I have the dubious distinction of being named after Omar Bradley, the World War Two general under Eisenhower during the European campaign. My mother fell in love with him—from afar, of course. Were you named after anyone special?"

"The moon," she answered. "That's what Cynthia means in Greek." She'd looked it up in a name book once. "I don't know what Louise means."

"Cynthia Louise?"

"Cindy Lou for short," she said with a southern accent, "if you're from Texas." And Sindee, if you were an exotic dancer. But she didn't say that.

"Was your mother fascinated with astronomy?"

The only thing her mother had been fascinated with was a bottle of liquor. "No," she murmured. "Not really."

"Tell me about your parents."

Brad Jordan approached things so casually, spoke of things so easily. Cindy felt her stomach start to churn with anxiety. She didn't want to talk about her parents. She didn't want to talk about her past. She didn't want to talk about *anything* personal. "There's not much to tell," she said with forced brightness. "They were my parents."

There was a brief pause during which his eyes never left her face. For a moment she thought he wasn't going to drop the subject. Then he glanced at his watch. "All you had was an hour for lunch?"

"Yes, is it late?" Surprised that time had fled so quickly,

she glanced at her own watch. "I have to get back to the clinic."

"And there are a few things I have to do." He stood to help her up. "Don't forget your fortune," he said when they were ready to leave. "I always keep mine. I tape it to the refrigerator for the hell of it."

"How many of them have you collected?"

"Lots. Truthfully, I use them to cover up the grease spots. I figure if the fridge is covered with little bits of paper, no one will notice the dirt."

She laughed, certain he wasn't as terrible a housekeeper as he pretended to be. When he handed her the fortune, she glanced at it and was surprised to read the usual, "You will achieve success in everything to which you aspire."

She looked up at him. Grinning, he shrugged in mock innocence. "So I made yours up. It didn't really say anything about me."

"But I saw the other fortune. It really said you'd meet a woman named Cindy. Did you have only one fortune custom-made?"

He laughed. "I didn't have *any* custom-made. It must be fate."

They had maneuvered their way through the restaurant and were standing near the exit, waiting by the cash register for a chance to pay. Brad had put his hand on her back to guide her. "Lunch was nice, wasn't it?" he said.

"Yes, it was very pleasant."

"Tomorrow we can go to a Mexican place I know."

Cindy paused. What was she going to do? She couldn't keep seeing him. After Peter, she'd decided not to let a man mess up her life again. "Brad, I don't think—"

"Oh, no," he cut in. "I won't let you say no. You have to teach me to dance, remember?"

"Brad—"

"I'll even learn the rumba," he interrupted again. "Do people do the rumba today?" Suddenly his features turned dark, and he shoved her quickly behind him. "Stay out of the way!" he warned.

"What?"

But Brad wasn't listening. His attention was riveted on a man standing at the cash register, holding a gun pointed at a waiter's head.

"Keep your hands where I can see them," the man said to the waiter. "Open the cash register real slow and hand me the money."

Everything happened so quickly that Cindy couldn't keep track of it all, but Brad had the advantage of surprise, as well as size and quickness. "Police," he ground out. Within seconds he had wrestled the gun from the man and slammed him up against a wall. "You're under arrest."

By then the restaurant crowd had erupted into bedlam. A woman screamed. A waiter dropped a tray. Two elderly women looked close to fainting, but another waiter got them into chairs and was efficiently calming them. Cindy, keeping out of the way, watched Brad with admiration. Quickly he handcuffed the robber and read him his rights, managing at the same time to exert a calming influence over the other patrons.

"Everything's fine, folks," he said. "Just a little attempted robbery here. Nothing to be concerned about." He shot a glance at the headwaiter. "Call for a squad car, please, and tell them to step on it," he ordered.

A squad car arrived quickly, pulling up out front. Two uniformed police officers burst into the restaurant, hands on their guns.

"The fun's already over," Brad told them, nodding toward his prisoner. "Take him in and book him. I'll be down later to do the paperwork."

Just like that, Cindy thought in awe as he walked over to her and took her arm. "You okay?"

"I'm fine," she said. She reached up to touch a scrape on his forehead. He must have been hurt in the scuffle with the robber. "But you really have a head injury now."

"Want to clean it for me?" He held out his handkerchief.

"We should go back to the clinic. Molly can take care of it better than I can."

"I'd rather you fixed it."

"She's a nurse."

"You're prettier." He sat down on a nearby stool and waited for her to administer first aid.

Cindy had to admit he had one hell of a line. "You know something, Brad Jordan? You're too charming for your own good." But she took his handkerchief anyway, dipped it in a glass of water that a waiter handed her, and dabbed at his forehead. The wound was superficial and would heal quickly. "I think you'll live."

"It's not a gaping hole?"

"Just a scrape."

"Too bad." They were close together, she in front of him. He slid his arms around her waist. "I hoped you might volunteer to take care of me forever and ever."

She gently extricated herself from his embrace. "I may be a soft touch, but I'm not a fool. And this is a public place," she added, glancing at the people watching.

"Too bad again." He laughed and stood up, taking her arm. "I guess we'd better go, before something else happens and I really get hurt."

Brad paid for their meal, and they headed back to the clinic. Cindy was glad they had eaten before the robbery. After all that activity, she wasn't certain she could enjoy a meal, even egg rolls. But apparently Brad handled similar incidents every day. He seemed completely relaxed as they strolled down the street.

"What are you doing tonight?" he asked.

"Tonight?" She was still thinking about their encounter at the restaurant.

"Actually around two in the morning, when I get off from work."

"Sleeping, I hope."

"Go to bed early," he advised. "I'll come by to see you then." They had arrived at the clinic doors, and he turned her in his arms to face him, brushing a lock of hair from her face. "Cindy? Look at me." The words were soft and husky as he bent over her. "You have the nicest lips."

Then his mouth met hers, and stars streaked through the noonday sky. "I suppose you did that because your head hurt," she murmured when he drew back slightly.

"No, I just wanted to kiss you," he answered. "But it hurts now. In fact, I feel a major relapse coming on."

As he leaned down to kiss her again, Cindy thought that surely she was going to faint. The stars zipping by started to explode, and the universe swirled around her in a kaleidoscope of colors. She melted against him, oblivious to the people walking by. Somebody snickered, and a teenager whistled, but Cindy couldn't have moved if she'd wanted to.

When he finally released her, Brad exhaled deeply. "Whew. I never realized being injured could be so much fun. See you later, babe. Don't wait up."

And then he was gone.

CHAPTER
Four

STUNNED, CINDY WATCHED as Brad slid behind the wheel of a sleek black Porsche and roared away. In a daze, she turned to go inside the clinic.

What in the world was happening to her? She felt as if a hurricane had just swept through her life and turned it upside down and sideways. Something had certainly wreaked havoc on her peaceful existence. Never had she felt so disoriented. To top it off, he'd called her "babe," a term she disliked, and she hadn't even had a chance to object.

The teenager who had snickered at them was waiting by the door. He was a tall, lanky kid with dark hair and a cleft in his chin. Standing so that he could flex his muscles, he grinned at her and held open the door. With her luck he would turn out to be her next client, Cindy thought, and she'd have to tolerate his snide remarks and knowing glances for the next hour. As much as she enjoyed working with teenagers, she was the first to admit that there were times when they could be unbearably obnoxious.

Nevertheless, she was still polite. "Thanks," she said.

"My pleasure, honey," the boy retorted with another grin. "Anything else I can do for you?"

The innuendo was hardly subtle. Cindy smiled at him, but without warmth. She wasn't certain what set her off, but for once, she wasn't going to put up with some snooty kid. "Yes," she said, "there is something you can do for me. Drop dead."

The boy laughed. "Wish I could, but I got an appointment with a Miss Cindy Marshall. She's going to keep me out of jail. You wouldn't happen to know her, would you?"

She opened her office door and gestured him inside with a sweep of her hand. "Come on in."

"Hey! All right! You it?"

"You got it."

All business now, she closed her office door and glanced at her calendar for his name. "Sit down, Michael, and if you want to stay out of jail, the first thing you need to do is learn when to shut your mouth."

"Uh, you talk, I listen?"

"Something like that."

He grinned. "I'm all ears, lady counselor."

Actually, he was mostly brawn. But Cindy just arched an eyebrow at him.

As the session progressed, Cindy found that it went much better than she had anticipated. Once he stopped trying to impress her with his sexual prowess, Mike was able to be quite open about his problems. In addition to failing in school, he had been arrested several times for petit larceny and once for possession of stolen goods. Nothing too bad—yet. But if things continued, he was bound to end up in a juvenile detention home. The judge had recommended counseling.

Cindy went one step further and recommended family counseling, though she doubted she would ever see his mother or father. If they did come in, at her insistence, she doubted they would understand the problems confronting their son. According to Mike, they were separated and so busy fighting over the children and blaming each other for their failed marriage that they had completely lost sight of how their behavior was affecting their family. She wondered what they would do if Mike ended up behind bars or got his girl friend pregnant. They would be shocked, probably, and furious—with him and with each other—but it would probably never occur to them that the entire episode might have been prevented by merely listening instead of trying to place blame. In the meantime...

She sighed and called in her next case.

The rest of the afternoon passed quickly. Five o'clock came and went before Cindy realized it. She went home exhausted, her thoughts still on her cases, particularly on Mike and Nicole.

Sometimes she felt so helpless. Sometimes, no matter what she did, she seemed bound to fail. Sure, she had talked to both kids, opened the lines of communication and made the proper recommendations—a foster home for Nicole and group counseling for Mike—but would any of it help? Would anything help?

She was almost at her door when a police car sped by, sirens screaming. Suddenly she remembered Brad Jordan. He would be coming to her apartment after his shift—at two in the morning.

But after a bit of good-natured teasing from Molly, Linda, and Darlene, Cindy had decided she wouldn't see him tonight. It would be far too dangerous to allow him to penetrate her defenses. She'd been hurt too many times already.

Yet she hadn't considered how she could prevent his visit. Unless she planned to sleep in the park tonight, she could hardly avoid him. She supposed she could call the police station and leave a message for him, but which station? A city the size of Chicago must have hundreds of precincts. She could simply refuse to answer her door. She could keep her lights off and pretend she wasn't home. But then he might think she was asleep and keep knocking, which would wake up her neighbors.

Or she could answer the door and tell the truth—that she didn't want to spend time with him. Simple.

Sure. *Nothing* was simple anymore.

The evening passed more slowly than the afternoon. Margie came over to visit, but left early, muttering that some people were terrible company. Cindy apologized, but she *was* distracted. What was she going to do about Brad Jordan? Besides, she saw Margie nearly every night.

After her friend left, Cindy took a shower. She had decided that the best course of action was to go to bed. If she waited up for Brad, she might seem anxious. And he might not even show up, she reasoned.

After all, why should Brad Jordan pursue her? He could probably have just about any woman he wanted, so why Cindy Marshall? There was nothing special about her—except maybe her past. Now, that *was* extraordinary. Not many people could boast of having glued a gold coin in their belly button and strutted down a runway wearing nothing much but chains.

To her credit, Cindy had left behind all that. She'd risen above her past and made something of her life. She had an education, a good job, friends, and five cats.

She flicked water at two of the kittens who were batting playfully at the shower curtain. "Scat!" she said as she stepped from the tub. They both scampered off into the other room.

Cindy laughed at their antics as she toweled herself dry and slipped on her best nightgown, a slinky peach-colored creation that Margie had given her for her birthday. Long and form-fitting, it flowed around her ankles in a silky swirl, making her feel special. She smiled at her reflection in the mirror. Now all she needed was a bit of makeup.

Good grief, what was she doing? She was dressing up for Brad's visit! Worse, her heart was pounding in excitement! What was the matter with her? A man was coming to her apartment—one of the sexiest, most attractive men she'd ever met—and she was wearing a gown that revealed so much cleavage she could have put Jezebel to shame. She'd told herself she wasn't going to let him in, but who was she trying to fool? Nobody *slept* in a gown like this one!

Quickly she peeled off the frothy garment and dug out her oldest and ugliest nightgown, a faded blue flannel with pink and green flowers decorating the neckline. She topped it off with a chenille robe of deep maroon that had seen far better days. One pocket was ripped entirely off, several threads were pulled, and the robe was so thick that Margie had once joked that even a bullet couldn't penetrate it.

Hopefully, neither could Brad Jordan. So what if it was the middle of July, and the temperature was in the high eighties? A little sweat never hurt anyone.

Fully armored, Cindy sat on the living-room sofa. Feeling restless moments later, she got up and turned on the television set, surprised when the news flashed on the screen. She checked her watch. Was it only ten o'clock? She was in for a long night. She sighed and picked up a magazine. One of the cats meowed and cuddled against her.

Cats! Sitting up straight, she gazed around her at the apartment. Good lord, she couldn't have company! The place was a disaster. The curtains were still tied up, and the covers on the furniture hung askew. The tables were bare and dusty. Brad had joked about his own poor housekeeping, but if he saw her living room he would think she was a hopeless slob.

"Don't you come near these," she admonished the cats sternly as she pulled down the drapes and shook them out. Clearly, it would take more than a flick of the wrist to get rid of the wrinkles. She headed for the closet where she kept her iron.

At two o'clock, Cindy finished cleaning her apartment. After vacuuming and dusting, she'd taken the covers off the furniture and steam-ironed the curtains. She'd even put out several of her favorite plants and some decorative pillows with long, attractive fringe.

For once, the cats were behaving well. Sam, the mother, was sleeping, curled up in her favorite spot on the sofa, and the kittens sat in a row, heads cocked, watching curiously as Cindy scurried back and forth putting cleaning supplies away.

Finally she paused and surveyed the room. She might not get a certificate in interior design, but at least her apartment looked neat and clean.

She sat down on the sofa. By now her pulse was pounding furiously in her throat. Adrenaline surged through her body. If her heart kept up this rhythm, she would end up in intensive care. And the man wasn't even here yet! What would she do when Brad Jordan actually knocked on her door? Would he even come?

By three o'clock she'd chased the cats away from the curtains at least ten times. She changed the channel on the television set, wondering how long she'd watched the test pattern before realizing it. The darned things were still broadcast in black and white. She stifled a yawn. She would be exhausted tomorrow.

She was exhausted already. Maybe Brad wasn't coming.

Right. Wishful thinking. He was coming, all right. He didn't strike her as the type of man *not* to show up.

Maybe she should go to bed.

She sighed. She'd never get to sleep. She was too nervous.

Cindy stifled another yawn and pulled all the kittens onto her lap, curling up with them so she could rest her head on a pillow. She'd lie down for just a moment.

It seemed that she'd barely closed her eyes when she woke, startled, to the sound of knocking on her door. She sat bolt upright. Was it him? Why hadn't he used the downstairs buzzer? That was the disadvantage of living in a building where the outside door was left unlocked. People could easily get into the building. But her landlord didn't see the sense in installing locks downstairs, insisting that when tenants moved out, he would have to change them.

The knocking continued, and Cindy stumbled sleepily to the door. "Who is it?"

"Brad." The single word was soft, muffled by the thick wood.

Now what should she do? She pulled her robe tighter around her body and glanced in a nearby mirror. She looked like a witch on Halloween! All she needed was a broomstick. Her long blond hair was sticking up at odd angles, and the maroon robe, aside from being tattered and shapeless, made her look as pale as a cadaver. Of course, Brad probably looked as sexy as hell.

"Cindy?" he called softly.

"Yes?"

"Aren't you going to let me in?"

She wanted to say no, but she pulled open the door. Sure enough, Brad Jordan stood there, one arm propped casually against the wall, looking absolutely gorgeous. His hair was tousled, falling over his forehead in an appealing slash, and light stubble shadowed his face. His shirt was open, and his mirrored sunglasses dangled from a breast pocket.

It was odd how some men had *bedroom* written all over them, she thought, even when they weren't near a bed. Brad Jordan not only exuded sex appeal; he screamed disaster. Instead of taping his fortune to the refrigerator, he should paste caution signs all over his body: *Sharp curve ahead. Danger, man at large.* Or better yet, *Stop!*

"Hi," he said.

"Hi," she answered, trying to smile. She should tell him to go home. She should tell him she didn't want to see him, that she used to be a stripper, that she was sleepy, hungry, had contracted a dread disease—anything, just so he would leave! Alarms went off in her head, loud bells warning her to beware, but she just stared at him.

"Got any tea?" He held up a small brown paper bag. "I brought egg rolls. You said you could eat them twenty-four hours a day. Were you asleep?"

"Yes." After all, it was three-thirty in the morning. But what did it matter if he knew she'd waited up for him? "Actually, I had just drifted off."

He nodded at her robe. "Are you cold?"

She followed his gaze. How silly she must look! And how obvious—never mind how ugly. She would have been better off wearing the sexy gown Margie had given her. "I felt a draft."

He nodded knowingly. "There *is* a lake breeze."

"Mm-hm."

He grinned again, and she heard the warning bells in her head clang louder. "May I come in?"

The bells went wild: *Say no! No, no, no! Tell him to go away before it's too late!* But Cindy just stood aside and opened the door farther. "Oh, I'm sorry. Yes, please come in."

She turned around, and more bells seemed to go off.

Actually, the sound she heard wasn't a bell but a frantic meow followed by a clunk as a plant crashed to the floor. Sparky streaked across the room, heading for cover.

Cindy stared in dismay at her apartment. It resembled a war zone! With a sinking feeling, she realized she'd been the only one sleeping. The kittens had been busy destroying her apartment! And she'd hoped to impress Brad with her housekeeping abilities?

The pretty pillows she'd placed on the sofa had obviously been the object of a tug-of-war, and all the bric-a-brac she'd set on tables had been overturned and investigated. A lampshade was askew. Other plants had been knocked over. Part of the drapes had been pulled off the curtain rod. How had she slept through it all?

"Sasha, get down!" she shouted as one of the kittens scampered to the top of the drapes.

At the sound of her sharp tone, the others scurried into corners and under chairs—all of them except their mother, whom Brad scooped up in his arms. "Is this Sam?"

"Yes."

"She looks like a nice lady."

That was exactly the impression Cindy had first had of the cat. Except she'd thought Sam looked like a gentleman. And both impressions had gotten her into her present trouble. "She is a nice lady," Cindy said as she went to pry Sasha off the curtains, "but her kittens are little devils."

She righted a plant and placed it on a high shelf, out of harm's way. Some dirt had spilled on the floor, but at least the leaves were intact. No real damage had been done.

Brad laughed and scratched Sam's ears. "I gather kittens eventually grow out of their devilment?"

"Eventually." Seeking out the kittens under the furniture, Cindy gathered them in her arms, introducing them as she went. "This is Jilly," she said, indicating the gray cat. "And Sasha and Delilah." She held out a calico, and a black-and-gray striped kitten. "Sparky is the only male, and he's fascinated by things that sparkle."

"What does he do with them?"

"He hoards them, unless I catch him."

Brad reached out to take Sparky from her. "What can we do to make them settle down for a while?"

"I'll give them their vitamin supplement. It comes in the form of an ointment," she explained. "You know how cat's hate to be dirty. When I want them to sleep for a while—usually at night—I rub some vitamin ointment on their paws. They start to lick it off and get involved in cleaning themselves, which tends to tire them out."

"Sounds complicated."

"But it works. Do you have any pets?"

"No, no attachments."

"Did you have a busy night?"

"Always."

"Did you..." She paused, searching for the proper word. "Bust anybody?"

He laughed at her use of the street term. "Three or four people. We made a drug bust. Had a wild car chase, just like in the movies."

Busy was beginning to sound like an understatement, particularly if one considered this afternoon's robbery. "Are you all right?"

"Just fine. A little tired."

Now that she was looking more carefully, she saw that the lines around his eyes were a bit deeper than they had been this afternoon. Unaccountably, she wanted to soothe and comfort him. She wanted to massage his shoulders and stroke her hand across his forehead. She wanted to kiss him and make it better....

"Cindy?"

"Yes?" Quickly she pulled her attention back to the

Naughty and Nice 67

present. She had to stop this daydreaming. For a moment she'd thought she *had* moved to touch him, and from his grin, she knew he'd read her thoughts.

"The egg rolls are getting cold. Do you have that tea?"

"Oh, sure." Glad to get away from him, she took Sparky from him and headed for the kitchen, thinking he would wait in the living room. But Brad followed, carrying Sam, whom he petted and stroked as he glanced around her apartment.

Cindy's apartment wasn't elegant by any stretch of the imagination; she lived in a three-room flat consisting of a kitchen, bedroom, and living room. But she had decorated with bold colors, and her kitchen was bright. Stark white walls and yellow appliances contrasted with lots of green plants, which she'd just put back out tonight and which thankfully, the kittens hadn't attacked. She'd have to clean up the mess in the living room later. At the moment she needed to calm down her animals.

She rubbed the ointment on their paws. Horrified, they ran into a corner and immediately started licking it off. Still carrying Sam in his arms, Brad sat down at the small glass-and-chrome table. "You have a nice place here."

"Thanks." She put the teakettle on a burner and got out two plates for the egg rolls, then leaned against the counter to wait for the water to boil.

Brad was still petting the cat. Watching him stroke the silky fur back and forth, back and forth, she suddenly wished she were sitting in his lap instead, that his hands were stroking her, down her back, along her thighs, across her breasts.

She took a deep breath and shifted uncomfortably.

"Are you still feeling a draft?" he asked.

"No, not anymore." Incongruously, Cindy felt herself blush. What she'd been feeling was hardly a draft. She must have trembled. And judging by his knowing grin, he must have guessed what she'd been thinking. Again!

"The water's boiling," he said.

So am I, she wanted to shout. But she turned quickly around. "So it is."

She poured hot water into the teapot, then got out a lemon and very meticulously cut it into slices, grateful to have something physical to do. Yet the heat didn't dissipate from her body. She could feel his gaze on her, his eyes watching her as she moved from the refrigerator to the counter to the table. Margie was wrong; bullets *could* penetrate the robe. His caressing gaze made her feel naked.

She took another deep breath. "Sugar?"

"Just lemon," he answered. When she finally sat down, he said, "Tell me about your job. How's a girl who lives on the North Side end up working at a clinic in downtown Chicago?"

Brad's tone seemed to imply that the Crisis Center was located in Alaska. "I have a friend whose husband is the state's attorney," she said. "He gave me a recommendation after I graduated from college."

"You know Steven Wade?"

"Yes, I do." Cindy smiled. "Do you know him?"

"I know *of* him, and I've met him in court once or twice when I've testified for a case. Seems like a nice guy."

"He is. Do you go to court often?"

"Quite a bit, actually. Nick and I have a big caseload."

She stirred her tea thoughtfully. "You really like your job, don't you?"

"Except for the paperwork." He grinned. "Nick and I drew straws tonight to see who'd have to stay late and type the reports."

"Who won?"

"Me, but I cheated."

"Brad!"

"Don't worry, Cindy, Nick cheats, too. It's a little game we play—when we can't get a rookie to type them for us."

"A female rookie, I'll bet."

His grin broadened. "Hey, it's a tough life down at the station house."

Sure. Being propositioned twenty-four hours a day had to be rough. And after seeing how her friends had reacted to him, she was certain he got propositioned all the time. "What was your car chase tonight all about?"

"Oh, that." He leaned back comfortably in his chair, locking his hands behind his head. "It could have been a scene from a Hollywood movie. We chased this guy all the way down the Outer Drive. He was up on the embankment half the time, or bouncing off the curb. We finally caught up with him when he turned off at Thirty-first Street. He thought he was in outer space, being chased by aliens."

"What'd you do with him?"

"Took him to the hospital. When we got to the emergency room, he remembered that his wife was locked in the trunk of the car. When we let her out, she thanked us, then shot us with her laser gun."

"Do you mean with a real gun?" Cindy asked, aghast.

"No, it was a squirt gun. She soaked Nick."

Cindy laughed, but she couldn't help being concerned about the couple. Brad shook his head, too, as he told her about another case. Although she knew he was leaving out most of the gory details, she chuckled at his description of the housewife who had hit him over the head with a pot when he'd tried to arrest her husband! She couldn't help laughing over the drunk who had passed out in the back seat of his Porsche. Before she realized it, several hours had passed, and they had finished drinking an entire pot of tea.

"Enough cop talk. Are you from Chicago?" he asked

when she'd boiled some more water and sat back down.

"No, I grew up in Boston."

He seemed surprised. "You don't have an accent. Don't tell me you're a proper Boston Brahmin."

"Hardly. I lived in downtown Boston, near an area known as the Combat Zone."

"Isn't that the red-light district?"

"Yes, among other things."

"I always thought that was a strange name."

"It's a strange neighborhood."

"Growing up there must have been rough."

"Yes, it was. Very rough." She thought about her childhood for a moment. "Loud, too. I remember there were rows and rows of bars along the street I lived on, and music played day and night. Everybody was poor. No one had any money, yet they all drank."

"Is the area still there?"

"Probably. I haven't kept track."

"When did you move away?"

She paused and started to fidget with her napkin. Few people knew about this part of her past, and she preferred not to talk about it even with Brad. "I left when I was fourteen."

"Is that when you came to Chicago?"

Thank goodness he hadn't asked about her family. Did he sense that it was an uncomfortable subject for her? "I didn't come straight here," she said. "I went to Texas and stayed there for a while."

For most of her childhood and teenage years she'd been looking for love—in all the wrong places. When she decided to run away for good, after her father beat her, she left Boston with a stranger she picked up on the street. After he dumped her in North Carolina, she hitchhiked south until, out of money, she jumped a train and rode the rails to Galveston. There she made her living as a go-go dancer in a bar. She ended up in Chicago by accident a few years later. One night she got in a car with another male "friend" who suddenly decided he wanted to see Lake Michigan.

"Texas?" Brad's remark brought her back to the present. "That's right. I forgot. You did tell me that this afternoon. But you don't have a Texan drawl either."

"Oh, no?" she said. "Y'all oughta hear me talk Texan. An' I can tell some tall tales, too."

Brad laughed. Whether by instinct or by intellect, he seemed to sense that she didn't want to discuss the subject further. "You must have a nice view," he said. Sam jumped off his lap and went to investigate more interesting areas of the apartment. The kittens were still curled in a corner, sprawled over each other, sleeping. "You're close to the lake," Brad remarked, strolling to the window.

Cindy couldn't see Lake Michigan from her apartment. It was several blocks away, and she wasn't high enough to see over the other buildings. Her view was really of the street, but if she looked kittycorner, she could see the trees that lined Lake Shore Drive. Beyond the road was the beach bordering Lake Michigan.

She glanced outside and was shocked to realize that the sun was coming up over the horizon. They'd talked that long? Brad also seemed amazed. They stood in the window watching as red streaks fanned out in the sky.

"It's beautiful, isn't it?"

"Yes," she said softly.

"It's prettier by the lake."

"I think everything is prettier by the lake."

"Do you like the beach?"

"I love it. I used to love the ocean, too—the endless water, the waves lapping to shore."

"You've never thought about moving back to Boston?"

She shrugged. There was nothing in Boston for her except reminders of her unhappy childhood. Sometimes she wished she knew what had happened to her parents, but more often she preferred not to remember them at all. "No, I like Chicago."

"Even though it's cold?"

"Boston's cold, too. And Chicago's not always cold. Sometimes it's hot, like now."

"True." He had moved closer, and suddenly he tilted her chin so that she was looking up at him. "Cindy?"

"Yes?"

Brad didn't answer. Instead he kissed her, softly, gently, his lips moving commandingly across hers. Every cell in her body came tinglingly alive. Despite her silent objections, Cindy didn't want the embrace to end. Apparently neither did he, for he sighed as he lifted his mouth. "I hope you don't mind. My head hurt, and I needed a quick kiss to make it feel better."

"I'm beginning to think you're a hypochondriac," she answered softly.

"No, hypochondriacs have all sorts of ailments. I have only one." He traced the outline of her mouth with one finger. "Did I tell you that you have nice lips?"

He had nice everything. "Yes, earlier today."

He sighed again. "Too bad."

Cindy frowned. "About what?"

"Since the sun's coming up, you have to go to work."

She knew at once what he meant. If she didn't have to go to work, there were lots of other things they could do.

"Yes, I do have to go to work."

"I'll be glad to give you a lift. I should stop by the station house anyhow, and it's close to the clinic."

"When will you sleep?"

"Later." He shrugged. "After I clear the magazines and pizza cartons off my bed."

She smiled. "Do you want some breakfast? I could make us eggs."

"Tell you what, you go get dressed, and I'll whip up the breakfast."

"All right." She hesitated only a moment. For reasons she couldn't explain, she trusted him implicitly. Maybe it was his slow and easy approach. Although he'd kissed her, he certainly wasn't rushing her.

A few minutes later, when she glanced at her reflection in the bathroom mirror, she decided that Brad was crazy to have wanted to kiss her at all! She looked terrible! It was amazing he hadn't run away when she'd first answered the door. In addition to her hair being mussed, mascara was smeared beneath her eyes. The maroon robe not only made her look pasty; it clashed with the blue, pink, and green of her nightgown. She laughed. Instead of being a sight for sore eyes, she would make someone's eyes sore.

When Cindy emerged from her bedroom thirty minutes later, Brad had fried some bacon and started to cook eggs and toast bread. And he'd fed the cats, who were wide awake and chasing each other's tails, tumbling all over one another. Brad seemed to like them. He was talking softly to them as he moved around her kitchen.

Cindy paused in the doorway for a moment to watch him. Even with a pancake turner in his hand, he looked totally masculine. He was tall and broad-shouldered, but even more than that, he was completely relaxed and comfortable in his role—whether it be as cook, confidant, or cop. She might even enjoy being arrested by him, she thought with a smile.

"Can I help?" she asked, coming into the room.

"You look nice." He turned to appraise her, and she felt her heart lurch in response to his bold gaze. She had to get hold of herself. As nonchalantly as possible she went to the refrigerator.

"Thanks. I have some homemade jelly for the toast."

"You made it?"

She nodded, placing it on the table. "I made only a few jars." And that had taken her hours—cooking the grapes, straining the juice. "I have one jar left." She went to a cabinet to get plates. When she turned around, Delilah had leaped onto the table and was balancing on the edge, one foot in front of the other like a tightrope walker. "Scat!" Cindy said. "Get off the table."

Startled by her voice, the kitten lost its footing and tumbled off the edge. For a moment Cindy thought she was watching a vaudeville comedy skit in super-fast motion. The cat became a blur of paws, claws, and fur as it sailed to the floor, taking with it the jar of jelly, which shattered on impact. To Cindy's amazement, the cat landed upright on all four feet, several inches away from the broken glass.

"Looks as if he likes sticky things, too," Brad said quietly from beside her as Sparky, always the curious one, crouched at the edge of the mess and began to sniff the jelly.

Cindy stared at the messy purple blob on the floor. So much for impressing Brad with her culinary expertise. She sighed and cleaned up the sticky mess. "I hope you like butter on your toast."

"Actually, I love butter on my toast," he said, chuckling until Cindy couldn't help but join in.

Breakfast went as well as could be expected with the kittens running back and forth, investigating every nook and cranny of her apartment. Until now, she hadn't realized what a pain they could be. Before she left for work, she tied her curtains back up and put covers on the furniture after stowing her breakable knick-knacks in a closet.

Once outside, Brad helped her into his Porsche. As soon as he started the engine he turned on a police radio, which crackled with reports of ongoing business the entire time they drove. Evidently Chicago was a busy place.

"How can you understand what they're saying?" Cindy asked a few moments later. Everything seemed to be broadcast in a strange code.

Naughty and Nice

"You get used to deciphering the jargon."

"Why don't you have to listen all the time?"

"If headquarters wants me, they'll give me a call or buzz my beeper. I listen to the calls on the radio just in case anything goes down nearby."

"So you can join the chase?"

He shot her a quick grin. "The chase is the fun part."

Really, now? But Cindy didn't say anything. She relaxed against the plush upholstery and tried to listen to the calls, but they sounded like glibberish to her. She gazed out the window. Despite rush-hour traffic, Brad pulled up in front of the clinic in record time.

"Don't try to park," she said. "I can get out here. Thanks for the ride."

"No problem." He reached across to open her door. "Catch some sleep this evening, okay? I'll come by to see you when I get off from work."

At two or three in the morning again? For a moment she hesitated. She should tell him she couldn't see him anymore. She should run the other way. She should do a lot of things, but she didn't do any of them. Instead she nodded. "Okay."

"Cindy?"

"Yes?"

"I thought you might like to know, my head hurts, and only one thing will ease the pain."

"That's getting to be an old ploy, Brad." She laughed and swung out of the car before he could lean over to kiss her. "Maybe you'd better buy another bandage," she added as she closed the door and peeked through the window. "Bye."

"You've got a mean streak in you, Cindy Marshall." But he laughed and waved as he pulled the car away.

CHAPTER
Five

THE CLINIC WAS always busy on Thursday, and today was no exception. Cindy acquired four new cases, all of them young teenagers, two of whom were totally flipped out on drugs and had to be admitted to the hospital.

Sometimes her job was so damned frustrating. There were moments when she wanted to shake the kids until they realized what they were doing to their lives. There were moments when she wanted to point to herself and say, "Don't mess up like I did. Don't do things you'll regret later."

She sighed. Her exhaustion didn't help her mood. She wasn't accustomed to going for over twenty-four hours without sleep, and she found it difficult to function, let alone be alert, interested, and enthusiastic. The entire day had turned out to be a downer.

Then, too, her common sense had returned, and with it, her natural inclination toward self-preservation. Although she felt like a light bulb where Brad Jordan was concerned—one moment on, the next moment off again—she'd analyzed her life very carefully and had decided not to see him anymore.

Yet, over and over again she'd told herself how dangerous he was, and the moment he'd shown up last night, she'd thrown caution to the wind. What was the matter with her? She must be experiencing a bout of temporary insanity.

Yet all day she'd half expected to look up and find Brad lounging nonchalantly in her doorway, grinning at her, his eyes twinkling from behind those darned sunglasses. She had to admit she'd have been delighted to see him. No doubt she'd have fallen all over herself, blushing and twittering like a teenager. His head hurt, indeed!

When five o'clock ticked by without a sign of him, she was almost relieved. Now all she had to do was figure out how to get out of their date tonight.

She walked quickly to the elevated train. First she had to get home without falling asleep.

Thirty minutes later, Cindy yawned as she pushed open her apartment door. Immediately, the cats came running, all meowing loudly. They were probably hungry. Her cats were *always* hungry. Sam led the way into the kitchen, the others following.

After she fed the cats, Cindy stared at the phone. Now what? She'd spent the night with Brad Jordan, in a manner of speaking, but she still didn't know his phone number. She yawned again. Perhaps that was just as well. She needed some rest. Funny how something as simple as sleep could suddenly seem so welcome. She could easily slide between the sheets and sleep for the next ten years or so.

She headed for the bedroom, vowing to worry about Brad Jordan later.

Naughty and Nice

But she had just changed into a pair of pajamas when her doorbell buzzed from downstairs—three long rings and two short ones, Margie's signal.

"Oh, no," she groaned, suddenly remembering. This was Thursday and every Thursday evening she and Margie did volunteer work at the retirement home, playing checkers with the elderly residents, reading them books and magazines, or just visiting with them. She sighed and went to answer the door.

Margie swept into the room, dressed in another flamboyant red outfit, this time a slinky jumpsuit that clung to her shape as if it had been glued in place. Cindy smiled. The old men wouldn't be lethargic tonight. But then, they never were when Margie was around. She kept them laughing and having a grand ol' time.

"Look what I brought you," Margie announced, holding out four yellow laundry baskets. "One for each of the little devils."

"For the kittens?"

"Are there any other devils in your life?"

"Thanks, but what am I supposed to do with these?"

"A customer who came in the store today told me that if you turn the baskets upside down and put the cats underneath them, the little suckers can't figure out how to get out."

"That sounds cruel."

"Oh, hell, it's not cruel. You're only going to put the cats in once in a while, like in the evening when I come over." Margie gave Cindy an assessing glance, focusing on her pajamas. "Hey, are you sick?"

"No," Cindy answered, "I'm just tired. I forgot tonight was Thursday."

Margie glanced at her watch. "You must be *really* tired. It's only six o'clock! Didn't you sleep last night?"

"No," Cindy admitted, "not very well."

"Why not?"

She could hardly tell Margie about Brad. The buxom redhead would tease her mercilessly, and demand a blow-by-blow account of every single moment Cindy had spent with him. Besides, Margie disdained cops more than Cindy did, and she would have a stroke if she found out Cindy was dating one, even casually. She shrugged. "I don't know. I just couldn't sleep."

"Since when? You usually sleep like a dead person."

Why was Margie making such an issue of it? Cindy shrugged again. "I just couldn't sleep."

"Cin-dy?" Margie said her name slowly in a singsong voice, like a little kid who'd caught her friend in a lie. "Cindy, what were you doing last night?"

Cindy felt herself blush. Something about Brad Jordan must bring out the red in her. If she kept it up, she might turn that color forever. "Nothing."

"Come on, what were you doing last night?" Evidently guessing she'd hit on something, Margie pressed further. "Cin-dy, were you with a guy last night?"

"Of course not," Cindy said. Not in the sense that Margie meant. But she felt herself turn even redder.

Margie's grin widened until it was positively licentious. "You *were* with a guy! Cindy, are you seeing that blind man? I don't believe it!" she exclaimed. "You're seeing him!"

"He isn't blind."

"Right, I remember. He's gorgeous. Are you seeing him?"

"No, I'm not seeing him." She wasn't actually dating Brad Jordan. He had just come over for a friendly chat. There was nothing she could have done to prevent it.

But Margie was gleeful. "Then why are you so red-faced?"

"I think I'm catching the flu."

"You just finished saying you aren't sick. Tell me about him," she went on excitedly. "What's he like? Did you go to bed with him?"

"Margie!"

"Oh, hell, Cindy. You act like sex is a bad word. Even nice women sleep with guys when they get a chance, especially a guy who's gorgeous. So did you?"

"No, I did not sleep with Brad Jordan!" Cindy said emphatically. "I did not have a date with Brad Jordan, and I do not think sex is a bad word. Yes, I did see him, but all we did was talk, and I really don't want to discuss it." She tried to look stern. "Now, are we going to the retirement home tonight or not? If we are, I have to get dressed."

"Sure, let's go," Margie answered. "But I thought you were catching the flu," she added facetiously.

Cindy smiled. "As you pointed out, I just finished saying I'm not sick."

Margie stuck out her tongue, and Cindy laughed as she went to her bedroom to change. Even though she was tired, she didn't want to miss a visit to the retirement home. She felt a real commitment to the elderly residents.

"Oh," Margie called from the other room, "I meant to tell you, I saw old Peter Piper today. He was with some sweet-faced broad, a skinny little thing. I told him you were better looking."

Cindy grimaced. All she needed was Margie in her corner. "Thanks."

"You're welcome." Margie paused in the doorway. "By the way, he's still not worth what you went through over him."

Cindy nodded. "I know." And for the first time she realized she was thoroughly and completely over Peter Ryan.

Only Brad Jordan affected her now...

They were busy all evening, leaving Cindy little time to think about how tired she was. She played three games of checkers and two games of chess losing each one. Later, she read a magazine article out loud to two residents and discussed a recipe with a third. In the meantime Margie played the piano and led a group sing-along. Afterward, everyone gathered in the kitchen for coffee and rolls.

Promising to meet Margie on Saturday morning for a shipping spree, Cindy went home more exhausted than ever, but feeling uplifted nevertheless. She always got a good feeling when she visited the elderly residents.

Yawning, she changed back into her pajamas and slid into bed. Just lying down felt good. She checked her alarm clock. Eleven o'clock. If she skipped breakfast, she could get an extra half-hour of sleep in the morning.

Then she remembered: Brad Jordan.

Good Lord, he was coming by to see her after he finished work—tonight. Cindy chewed her bottom lip, trying to think. Finally she set her alarm clock for one o'clock. "After work" probably meant around two in the morning. She would get up, take a shower, and get dressed. She wasn't going to let him stay long, but it was only fair to tell him in person that she didn't want to see him again.

To Cindy's surprise, after her two A.M. shower, she felt refreshed, if not full of energy. She pulled on shorts and a tank top, and applied makeup sparingly. No sense getting dressed up; she was just going to take everything off again as soon as Brad left.

She didn't have to wait long for his knock. She had just finished dressing and was walking into the living room when he tapped once, lightly. She took a deep breath and went to answer the door. All she needed now was a good excuse.

And a lot of willpower, she added a few seconds later as he stood smiling in her open doorway, taking her breath away with his gorgeousness. Why couldn't she prepare herself for the sight of him?

Though, as usual, he was wearing a sports coat to hide his shoulder holster, he was dressed in tight-fitting jeans instead of slacks. A dark T-shirt stretched taut across his broad chest. He was so damned sexy, even in casual clothes. She felt her heart start to thud erratically. It wasn't fair that anyone could look so good, particularly at this ungodly hour.

"Hi," he said. "Ready to go?"

"Ummm, no," Cindy murmured, puzzled. "I'm not."

"You look fine. Yellow's a good color for you. I'm surprised. Most blondes can't wear it. Do you have a swimsuit on under your clothes?"

She shook her head. "Of course not," she said, wondering how he knew so much about blondes.

He frowned. "Didn't I tell you I had a surprise for you?"

"No."

"Well, I do."

"Do what?"

He laughed. "Have a surprise for you. Better go change. Unless... do you want some help? I'd be glad to assist."

"No!"

"That's too bad. I'll give you thirty seconds." He glanced at his watch. "Then I come in and help you. Better hurry."

"But—"

"No buts. Thirty seconds. That's half a minute."

"What's the surprise?"

"Cindy, if I *tell* you, it won't be a surprise. Twenty-nine, twenty-eight, twenty-seven—"

Seconds! He was counting seconds! If she didn't get moving, he would help her get dressed—or rather, undressed.

"Of course—" Suddenly his expression changed, and he looked positively devilish. "We could stay here. You could teach me to dance. The guys tell me there won't be any rumbas at the policemen's ball, just cheek-to-cheek."

That's all she needed, dancing cheek to cheek with Brad Jordan. "I'm going," she said, hurrying toward her bedroom.

"Twenty-seven."

"Count slower! I'm going!"

"Twenty-six. Twenty-five."

Cindy had changed and was in his car beside him before she remembered that she wasn't going to see him anymore. What had happened to her vow? It had flitted away, like rose petals in the wind.

The sleek Porsche hummed smoothly as Brad headed south on the Outer Drive toward downtown Chicago. She ignored the police calls crackling over the radio, concentrating instead on their surroundings.

At night the city was so vibrant. When she'd worked at Club Arnaud, and had finished work late, Cindy had always been surprised by the number of people who were up and about at that hour. Chicago never rested. Now, from a distance, the buildings loomed tall and stately, like ghosts in the night. Rows and rows of streetlights, like toy candles, illuminated the area with a bright glow. Neon lights blinked off and on, and cars zipped by, full of laughing, carefree people. A warm, balmy breeze off the lake shifted through her hair.

"Tired?" Brad asked.

"A bit," she answered. Cindy hadn't realized that she had sighed out loud. She turned to him. Even in the dark there was something magnetic about him, something exciting. She could see his classic features—the strong forehead, chiseled nose, sensitive lips. His jaw jutted out slightly, a sign of strength. His hands held the wheel firmly as he steered the car.

"Didn't you rest?" he asked.

"Some. Tonight was my evening at the retirement home. I slept a few hours afterward."

Naughty and Nice

"Were you busy at the clinic?"

"Thursdays are always busy. I'm glad I don't have to work this weekend. Weekends are always tough."

"Weekends are bad in my business, too. People get crazy then. I don't know why."

"Maybe from boredom. People don't have their usual responsibilities to keep them busy on weekends. Where are we going?" she asked when he turned off the Outer Drive at Michigan Avenue.

"You must be a Virgo," he answered. "You don't seem to like surprises."

She glanced at him, amazed that he had pegged her so accurately. Her birthday *was* in September, and she was a typical Virgo: both serious and practical. These days, according to Margie, she was too serious and practical. She didn't agree, but according to Margie, since she had once been flamboyant enough to strip on stage, she must have been born on the Leo-Virgo cusp or with Leo rising. Cindy didn't know exactly when she was born, and didn't much care. "Do you believe in astrology, too?" she asked.

"No. Where you're concerned, I'm just a good guesser."

She smiled. It was true. And then there was that fortune cookie to consider. If it hadn't been a custom-made fortune cookie, then maybe fate *was* conspiring to bring them together. But immediately she chided herself for entertaining such a ridiculous thought!

Brad pulled into a parking space and reached into the back seat to retrieve a blanket. "Come on."

Cindy got out of the car. "You're still not going to tell me where we're going?"

"Oak Street Beach." Brad took her hand and hurried her down the sidewalk. "I thought we'd watch the sunrise. You said you like the beach. Have you ever been to this one?"

"Once or twice," she said. By then they were walking

through the tunnel that led underneath the Outer Drive to the beach itself.

Oak Street Beach was well known. Compared to the other beaches in the city, it was a very small stretch of sand, but it was located near the Gold Coast, right off of the downtown area. Like a small oasis, it was set apart from the city by the road and from the other beaches stretching along the lakeshore by its elite status.

At the moment it was deserted, a tiny stretch of golden sand that had been cooled by the night air. Lake Michigan stretched before them, vast and blue, the lights of an occasional boat twinkling in the darkness. Brad spread out the blanket and kicked off his shoes. A few seconds later he glanced up at Cindy. "Aren't you going to take off your shorts?"

"You're serious about this?" she said. "This is your surprise? We're going swimming at Oak Street Beach?"

"Uh-uh, water's too cold. Let's just sunbathe."

Cindy stared at him as though he'd just turned into a crazy person. She gestured at their surroundings. "Brad, it's dark. There's no sun."

He glanced at the sky. "There's a moon. And the sun will be up around five."

"It's three in the morning."

He took off his jacket. "Dawn's only a couple of hours away. Look at it this way. You won't get burned."

"You're actually going to *sunbathe?*" she said incredulously.

"Cindy, that's what you do at the beach. Unless..." He peeled off his shirt and winked at her. "Do you have any other ideas?"

"Sorry, not one," she answered dryly.

He winked again. "Too bad."

Cindy tilted her head to the side to study him. Sometimes he was hard to read. She couldn't tell if he was putting her on or not. He seemed serious, yet she wasn't convinced. "Brad, is it okay for us to be here?" she asked. "The park is closed."

"No one will mind. In Chicago nobody pays any attention to what time the parks close. Ever been to Buckingham Fountain at night? There are people there twenty-four hours a day, even when the water's shut off."

"But there's no one else here," she pointed out.

He flashed her a devilish grin and stripped off his jeans, revealing skintight swim trunks. "That's the idea, Cindy. Besides," he added, "even if we do get caught, the cops will just ask us to leave. They won't bother to arrest us."

Well, that was some consolation. She'd been arrested before, and she had no intention of letting it happen again.

By now he was totally undressed except for his bathing suit, his clothes lying in a neat pile beside the blanket. Cindy stared at his swim trunks—or rather, at the physique surrounding the swim trunks.

Brad Jordan's body was magnificent, lean and hard, without an ounce of excess flesh. His chest was broad and liberally sprinkled with light hair that arrowed down into his waistband. His abdomen was flat and firm, his legs strong. To her eyes, even his toes looked well shaped.

"Come on," he said, flopping down on his stomach and patting the stretch of blanket next to him. "I'll let you rub some suntan lotion on me."

"Gee, thanks." Cindy glanced around. If people could see her now, they'd think she was out of her mind. Nevertheless, she started to peel off her tank top. Brad, she noticed, had turned his back on her, as if to let her undress in privacy.

"Tell me when I can turn around," he said. "Staring off into the darkness isn't very interesting."

Why had he turned his back? she wondered. Was it because he thought she was modest? He did have some old-fashioned ideas. Or was he waiting to get the full effect of what she looked like in a bathing suit? If so, she hoped she would live up to his expectations. She took a deep breath as she took off her shorts and stood silhouetted in the moonlight. "I'm ready."

The only swimsuit Cindy owned was a modest one-piece in pale yellow. But when Brad looked up at her, a shiver of awareness trembled up her spine. His narrowed gaze swept over her full breasts and hips, down to her toes and back up to dwell on her face.

"You're a very beautiful woman, Cindy Marshall," he murmured softly.

Feeling her body grow hot under his scrutiny, she bent down to rummage through his belongings. "Do you have that suntan lotion?"

"What, don't want to get burned?"

She was already burning—even without the sun.

She found the lotion and motioned for him to turn over on his stomach. After squirting cream on his back, she started to rub it in. "I'm sorry to break it to you, Mr. Jordan, but you can't get a sunburn without the sun."

"Then why are you putting lotion on me?"

To keep you from staring at me, she thought. Aloud she said, "I've heard that at three A.M., blond male cops are particularly susceptible to moonburn. Either that or nature might surprise us and the sun might come up in the next ten minutes."

"And here I was hoping you just couldn't keep your hands off me."

Feeling foolish for doing it, she nevertheless let her hands slide down his body in long smooth strokes. The lotion was moist, and his skin was warm. She moved her fingers across his shoulders and along his back, slowly stroking, kneading. His muscles were tight, and the tiny hairs on his arms prickled sensuously against her palms.

"You have such a swollen head, Mr. Jordan," she teased.

"True, but Cindy..."

The husky note in his voice thrilled through her, and she quickly caught herself. Touching him was producing a worse effect than his gaze ever had.

"All done," she said abruptly, ignoring his innuendo and flopping down on the blanket beside him. "Any more and you'll be greasy. The sand will start sticking."

But she soon discovered that lying down was another mistake, for Brad shifted position and leaned over her, picking up the bottle of suntan lotion. "Turnabout's fair play," he murmured.

Cindy steeled herself for the shock of his touch. Just the thought of his hands on her body was enough to make her temperature-regulating mechanism go haywire. At first the lotion was cold as he squirted it on her skin, and she jumped. Then he started to slowly massage her back. The calluses on his hands were rough against her softer skin, and the pressure of his lean, strong fingers plying the muscles of her back felt tantalizing. Every cell in her body screamed in awareness: *Touch me, touch me. Make love to me.* She took a deep, purging breath. She had to get away from him.

"Thanks," she said, turning quickly over.

Another mistake. Now they were face to face, his hand at her waist. His body so close to hers that they could have been one. For a moment she just stared up at him. Then he murmured, "You're welcome."

To Cindy, the simple, polite phrase had never sounded so sexy. His voice was low and husky, and she could hardly hear him, but she could tell that he was going to kiss her. Her breath caught in her throat as his lips lowered slowly to hers. His hand moved up to cup her breast. Her pulse quickened in response. "Brad."

"Yes..."

His lips met hers, at first soft, then harsher, demanding. Behind them, waves washed to shore in gentle swishes, back and forth, back and forth, like the porch swing in her daydreams.

The white picket fence. The Victorian dream house.

Cindy heard the soft sound of the waves as though in a trance, but the only thing she was aware of was the feel of Brad Jordan pressing against her. She moaned and arched against him, body to body, flesh to flesh. Her breasts, heavy and turgid, ached for his touch, and desire began to throb deep inside her.

"Brad," she whispered again.

With a husky groan he pulled her even closer. His tongue darted into her mouth, advancing and retreating in tiny thrusts. Cindy twined her fingers in his hair, welcoming the sensual invasion, meeting his tongue with her own.

Several raucous shouts, and the blast of a car horn coming from the Outer Drive brought them both back to their senses. Brad sighed and pulled away. "I guess smooching on the beach wasn't such a good idea after all. Too many distractions."

"And think how embarrassing it would be if a park attendant came along," she pointed out.

"Mmm. The ultimate distraction."

She smiled as he pulled her to her feet. She'd been as affected by the kiss as he had, but she hadn't shown it; she thought it would be fun to tease him. "Don't you want to lie here and watch the sunrise?"

"That's not what I want to do, and you know it."

"Well, if we don't do something soon, I'm going to fall asleep." Cindy gave an exaggerated yawn.

"Next you're going to wound me deeply by saying my company is putting you to sleep."

She laughed. "Maybe."

"You're going to regret that, Cindy Marshall," he

threatened. "We need someplace a bit more private." Another car roared past on the Outer Drive. "I've got it," he said. "Let's go for a carriage ride."

She glanced at him in puzzlement. And what an odd thing to suggest! A carriage ride wasn't private, though it would certainly be fun. For years the old-fashioned horse-drawn buggies had been a colorful feature on Michigan Avenue. Recently she'd heard the law had been changed, and the city had limited the range of the carriages. But when Cindy had worked at Club Arnaud she had watched the horses plod past all the time in warmer months. Despite the noise and traffic zipping past, it had looked so romantic to see a man and woman cuddled in the back, a liveried driver perched on the seat, the horses' hooves beating a steady clop-clop as the carriage moved slowly down the street. She'd always dreamed of taking a carriage ride... with a man who loved her.

But her practical streak reasserted itself. "Brad, at the risk of sounding redundant, it's after midnight."

"Are you about to turn into a pumpkin?"

"You're just full of old lines, aren't you!" she teased. "Okay, what's so significant about it being past midnight?"

"Carriages don't run at three in the morning."

"O ye of little faith. Put on your clothes, babe. One carriage ride coming up."

Cindy didn't know how Brad accomplished it, but less than an hour later she was climbing into a horse-drawn carriage that immediately headed down Michigan Avenue. The liveries weren't officially running, yet Brad had known where the stable was, and somehow he'd convinced the man in charge to meet them and take them for a ride.

After they'd ridden for several blocks, one of Brad's arms slung around her shoulders, he began to point out the sights, as if conducting a guided tour. "On your left is the Art Institute," he said. "The statues of the lions are a famous Chicago landmark. And on your right—"

Cindy laughed, interrupting his recitation. "I know that, Brad. I've lived here for more than ten years."

"What? You don't like my running commentary on the city?"

"I'm familiar with all the landmarks," she said, pointing out two statues on opposite sides of Congress Street. "There are the American Indians. Do you know what big mistake the artist made?"

Brad nodded. "He put American Indians on Arabian horses. Well, I guess he didn't do his homework." He twisted around. "We can see Buckingham Fountain from here."

Suddenly Cindy froze. Who cared about Buckingham Fountain when just up the block stood Club Arnaud? The realization dawned on her abruptly, like a bolt of lightning. They were gong to drive right past the nightclub!

Should she say it then? *Hey! Ever hear of Freya, the Viking warrior maiden? That was me.*

"And there's the Conrad Hilton," Brad went on, pointing out the elegant hotel.

"Yes." Here was a perfect opportunity to tell him about her past. But the closer they got to the club, the tighter Cindy's stomach knotted. *Say it!* her mind screamed. *Tell him!* The building loomed ahead, just a few feet away, flashing red and blue neon lights. "Oh, there's Club Arnaud," she murmured finally as the horse trotted past.

"So it is." Brad glanced briefly at the nightclub. "That's a landmark, too."

"Yes." She attempted a smile. Her heart was beating in her throat so fast she could hardly hear herself speak.

"I hear it's changed ownership."

"Really?" What had happened to Tony? Cindy was surprised he hadn't called her or Margie. Had he retired? Was he lounging on a beach somewhere, spending all his money? "Have...have you ever been there?"

"Can't say that I have, not to Club Arnaud," he answered. "But I went to some clubs like it once or twice when I was a rookie on vice."

"You went as a cop?"

"Uh-huh," he answered. "We go occasionally to make sure the owners aren't violating the law."

"Raids, right?"

He laughed. "Occasionally the vice squad will conduct a raid, but I never raided any of the clubs."

She screwed up her courage. "What . . . what exactly did you do at the club?"

"Looked around."

"At the dancers?"

He laughed again. "Yes."

"Oh."

"Cindy, I'm not blind, remember?"

She chewed her lip, totally forgetting to laugh. "What'd you think?"

"Of the dancers?"

"Yes." Could he tell her throat was dry and her voice was hoarse? Did he know how nervous she was?

"The dancing looked like hard work."

It sure was. Dancing five or six twenty-minute sets every evening took stamina. Lots of nights she'd gone home completely exhausted. "Did you ever arrest anybody?"

"I've arrested a lot of people."

"I mean strippers."

"Once or twice. Why?"

Why. The word was so offhand, so casual. Three little letters. All she had to say was: *Because I was arrested once or twice when I worked here.*

She watched the nightclub go by. Clippety-clop, clippety-clop, the horse's hooves pounded on the pavement. Lord help her, she couldn't say it. "No reason," she murmured.

"Cindy . . ."

"Yes?" Suddenly close to tears, she could hardly speak.

"Cindy, is something wrong?"

He was regarding her with an expression so sympathetic that it nearly sent the tears spilling down her cheeks. Would his sympathy and understanding turn to contempt the minute she told him the story of her past?

"You know, if something's wrong, whatever it is, I'll understand," Brad added.

Would he? He was a cop, and if that wasn't enough to make him condemn her, he was also a middle-class suburban male, with middle-class suburban mores. They'd known each other only a couple of days. Just two short days. And she'd been hurt so many times before.

"Cindy?" he asked again softly.

She forced a smile. "Nothing's wrong, Brad." Quickly turning in her seat, she pointed to a monument in the distance. "Isn't that the statue of General Logan?" She'd tell Brad about her past—she *would*—but later, when he knew her better and would be better able to understand.

For a moment she thought he was going to pursue the subject of Club Arnaud, but to her relief he turned to glance at the statue. "The Civil War hero? Yes, there's another statue of him in Logan Square. We'll go see it sometime."

Determinedly she produced another smile. "Okay." In a few moments the carriage turned down a side street to circle around and take them back to their starting point. Cindy wasn't certain how she managed it, but she chattered like a magpie during the ride back and all the way to her apartment, too.

"Would you like to come in for tea?" she asked after Brad had parked and escorted her to the door.

"If I do, you won't get any sleep before you have to leave for work."

"I am tired," she admitted.

He nodded. "I'm off today, or rather tonight." Like most detectives, Brad worked a rotating schedule and had very few weekends off. "I thought I'd clean up the apartment and invite a few people over. You know, have a barbecue, show you how to cook a hamburger. How about if I pick you up after work, around five?"

"Okay." How could she possibly decline his invitation now, with no ready excuse available? Later she'd have to come up with a way to get out of seeing him.

She had to cut the relationship off. Every moment she spent with him she came more and more under his spell, becoming more and more vulnerable.

"I use mesquite with the coals," he explained. "Have you ever tasted hamburgers grilled over mesquite?"

"Yes, in Texas."

"How about hamburgers with hot barbecue sauce?"

"Texas, too."

"Foiled by the Lone Star State. All right, how about hamburgers cooked over mesquite with hot barbecue sauce and Brad Jordan's special toppings?"

"I don't believe I've ever had that." She smiled. "Not even in Texas."

"Good. Then five o'clock it is. See you then." Very tenderly he leaned down and kissed her, brushing his lips across hers as lightly as a feather. "'Night," he said huskily, then turned and clattered down the steps.

"Good night," Cindy murmured, leaning against the door, trying to gather her wits. Lord, she had to stop fooling around and get hold of herself, and she had to do something about Brad Jordan.

But it was too late. He had already penetrated her defenses. In a few more days she'd be in love with him, head over heels in love.

She sighed and went into her apartment, ignoring the kittens and whatever damage they had caused, and went straight to bed. She felt like a zombie. It was close to five in the morning, hardly an opportune time to analyze her attraction to a man. And right now, she wasn't going to try!

CHAPTER
Six

THANK GOODNESS FOR Friday. Although the Crisis Center was open seven days a week, twenty-four hours a day, Cindy didn't have to work nights, and this was her weekend off. She was on call all the time for her cases, but she wouldn't acquire any new ones until Monday. She would have forty-eight hours in which to sleep, and at the moment that was a most pleasant prospect.

After Brad left early that morning, she'd gone to sleep instantly and slept until the very last moment, arriving at her office on the stroke of nine. Now the clock was ticking rapidly toward five.

Cindy yawned as she tucked a last folder into the file cabinet. Assuming he'd be on time, Brad would arrive at any minute to pick her up. This afternoon she hadn't felt up to analyzing her attraction to him any more than she had early that morning, but she had decided to at least have dinner with him. She would go to his apartment, eat a hamburger, and meet his friends. Then she'd go home and fall into bed.

Suddenly it dawned on Cindy that, where Brad Jordan was concerned, the order of her list could easily get confused. She might end up in bed before she went home! He was a devastatingly attractive man; and she was devastatingly attracted to him. Perhaps she shouldn't let herself be alone with him.

But they wouldn't be alone, she reminded herself. He was having a barbecue; he had invited other people. There was safety in numbers, wasn't there? She sighed again and closed the file cabinet. She was too tired to think. Anyhow, she had promised Brad she'd come.

In deference to the continuing heat wave, Cindy was wearing a sundress made of cool, crisp cotton. Not exactly dinner attire, but it would do for a cookout. As she gave her office a final glance to make certain she had cleared everything up, she smoothed the wrinkles from her skirt and grabbed her purse. All the weekend counselors were already on duty, and several of her co-workers were getting ready to leave, including Molly.

"You seeing that gorgeous hunk again tonight?" Molly called as Cindy crossed the lobby.

Every person who worked at the Crisis Center knew Cindy had gone to lunch with Brad Jordan. Everyone had noticed that for the past two days she'd been so tired, she'd walked around in a daze. She suspected that a great deal of speculation was buzzing through the clinic gossip mill.

Reluctantly she admitted to Molly, "I'm seeing Brad for dinner."

"Ooh-la-la! I wanted to give him more than a bandage Wednesday morning. The doc made me behave. Let me know if he needs intensive care. I'll be glad to brush up on my bedside manner."

Cindy laughed and slipped out the door. Molly was all talk, a happily married woman with a couple of kids, one of whom was just a toddler.

But Brad Jordan *was* handsome, Cindy admitted once again as his Porsche pulled to the curb and he started to climb out of the low-slung sports car to open the passenger door for her.

"Don't bother, I can manage." Cindy waved him back inside and got the car door herself.

"Hi," he said as she slid into the seat. He leaned over to give her a quick kiss, brushing his lips lightly over hers. "How was your day?"

"Not bad." Did he know how devastating his kisses were? Each time he touched her, even briefly, she felt tiny currents of electricity tingle through her body. "Things went well today, especially considering this is Friday," she managed to add, settling herself against the upholstery as he pulled into traffic. "And how was your day off? Did you prepare the hamburgers?"

"No. I made the mistake of going by the station house after I dropped you off this morning. Do you like kiwi fruit?"

"Yes. Why? Don't tell me that's the special topping you talked about for your hamburgers?"

He laughed. "No. But when I went to the supermarket, a gorgeous broad was making a sales pitch for kiwi fruit by cutting them up and giving out samples. I bought a few."

"A gorgeous broad?" Cindy repeated dryly. Good thing she wasn't an adamant feminist or she might be insulted by such language.

He grinned again. "Sorry, sometimes I slip. Some cute chick."

She laughed. "That's even worse."

"How about a middle-aged lady working in the produce department? That's who she really was. She sold me some strawberries, too. In fact, I've got a regular fruit salad in the back seat."

Cindy glanced over her shoulder. Grocery bags, packed to overflowing, lined the seat as well as the car floor. "What all did she sell you?"

"About everything in the store," he said. "I'm a bad shopper. I buy on impulse."

"Obviously." She retrieved a small can from the top of one bag. "Do you really like caviar?"

"No," he said, "but Sam will."

"Sam will *love* it," Cindy corrected. "You'll spoil her."

"Good." He shot her a quick glance. "The only other female I want to spoil is you."

Really? Cindy smiled, and adroitly sidestepped his innuendo by saying, "Don't forget Sam has four kittens."

Brad just laughed. "If you look, you'll find five cans of caviar. There's ice cream back there, too. How about grabbing our cones? I got you cherry vanilla. I hope you like it. Mine's rocky road."

"Brad, they've probably melted all over everything!"

"They're in a small freezer chest with dry ice." At her look of amazement, he added, "You just have to know the right ice cream stores."

Shaking her head in disbelief, Cindy found the case and got out the cones. Sure enough, they weren't even starting to melt. She handed him one. "Do you do this often?"

"Every day. I have a weakness for ice cream." He licked the cone. "And for pretty blondes." Lots of pretty blondes, she imagined. "Tell me, what's your favorite flavor?"

"Cherry vanilla."

His eyes widened in apparent amazement. "I'll have you know that was purely accidental."

"Sure," Cindy countered, but she laughed again.

They ate their ice cream and chatted about nonsensical things for the rest of the ride to his apartment. Brad lived on the North Side, too, right off the Outer Drive, close to Children's Memorial Hospital. Most of the buildings were older, only two and three stories high with gray stone facings. He pulled up in front of a newer low-rise building, shut off the engine, and grabbed several bags of groceries.

"Tell me, are you liberated enough to help me carry these bags, or do I have to make several trips? I might be tempted to leave what I can't carry."

"Why did you buy so much food?" Cindy complained as she grabbed the last bags and followed him up the front steps.

"Be glad I don't drive a station wagon," he called over his shoulder as he bounded up the stairs ahead of her to the second floor. "With a Porsche, I can't buy too much on impulse. Of course, a Porsche is hardly a family car."

"Hardly," she agreed.

What would it be like to own a station wagon with him? And to have his children? Did he like pink roses?

She gave herself a mental shake. No sense dreaming about those things.

"I'm just down the hall," he said.

She indicated her grocery bags by shifting them slightly. "I'm fine, but you're going to drop yours," she said, nodding at the sacks in his hands, which were beginning to slip. "If you have eggs, they'll break."

"Thanks for the warning, Cindy, but the eggs are in your bags, with all the other lightweight stuff. *I've* got all the heavy items." He stopped abruptly in front of a door. "Here we are."

Cindy was amazed that he managed to unlock his door without dropping anything, but he did, sweeping into the room and rounding a corner in one quick movement to set the groceries in the kitchen. She entered behind him, closing the door and glancing around.

They had entered a huge room, which he'd cleverly divided into several sections by strategically placing the furniture in clusters. The entire room was decorated in hues of brown and beige. The carpet was dark brown, and most of the furniture was either rattan or cedar with beige tweed upholstery. In the living room area, two large sofas faced each other across a low glass-and-gold-chrome coffee table. They were flanked by two chairs in the same tweed fabric. A stereo system on low shelves divided that section from the small dining area.

Tall, narrow mirrors, seamed with strips of white-stained cedar, covered an entire wall. On the opposite wall a bank of patio doors led onto a terrace. A large bunch of fluffy pampas plumes tucked in a corner added to the casual yet elegant atmosphere. In the other corner, separated from the rest of the room by a carved screen, was what appeared to be a sleeping area.

The place was basically neat, although a light layer of dust covered the tables and a few clothes were scattered helter-skelter: A pair of jeans, a shirt, and several socks graced the floor. Obviously Brad's apartment was well lived in—when he was home. She imagined he was so busy with his police work that he spent very little time here. What time he did have wasn't spent doing housework.

Brad emerged from the kitchen and took the groceries from her arms. He set the bags on the dining room table, then picked up an empty yogurt container and a sports coat, which he tossed over his arm. "I meant to have the apartment cleaned," he said, bending to retrieve some socks, "but I was at the station house all day."

"I really don't mind."

"I do. One of these days I'm going to hire a maid."

"Swedish?" she teased.

"Blonde, definitely blonde. In fact, you might apply for the position. Could I get you to give up social work?"

"There are days when I would consider it," she bantered back, "but I don't do windows."

"How about floors?"

"I'm great on floors." She nodded toward the groceries. "That bag is leaking. Shouldn't you put it in the kitchen?"

"It must be the Popsicles."

"Do you have a weakness for them, too?"

"Especially grape." He opened a closet door and tossed the socks and sports jacket inside. "Ignore that," he said, coming back and snatching up the leaking grocery bag. "I'll take care of it later. I better make the hamburgers, or we'll never eat."

Cindy followed him into the next room. The galley kitchen was small, compact, and very functional, but she didn't like the framed poster hanging on the wall—a cross-section of an orange, juice dripping from the ripe center. The decor of the main room, especially this poster, made her strongly suspect he'd hired an interior decorator to do his apartment.

"Who else is coming to dinner?" Cindy asked.

"Some police friends," he answered. "Nick, Katie, Wes, Sylvia, and a few guys from the task force." He opened the refrigerator and began tossing groceries inside. "Now, where's that kiwi fruit?"

But Cindy had turned absolutely still. Talk about a bombshell. She didn't know whom she'd expected him to invite, but certainly not police friends. She would feel as uncomfortable in his apartment with a bunch of cops as she had in a courtroom in front of the judge!

Brad glanced at her. "I hope you don't mind."

What could she say? *I can't meet your friends because there's an outside chance one of them might have arrested me a few years ago?*

"No," she murmured. "I don't mind."

"Good. I want you to meet everybody. Mom and my stepdad will be here, too. So will my sister and her husband, and my brother and his wife."

His whole family was coming! "That's good."

"They're leaving the kids at home, though," he added, obviously unaware of her distress. "You'll have to meet them some other time. Katie's pregnant—did I tell you that?"

Cindy shook her head. "I don't know who Katie is."

"Oh, sorry. She's my partner's wife. Since Nick is about to be a father any day now, he's been acting like a fool. Or worse than one, according to Katie. This morning he began a leave of absence from work, and he won't go back until after she delivers."

To Cindy that didn't sound the least bit foolish, more like a husband who was in love with his wife. "I think that's a nice thing to do."

"Oh, that's not bad," Brad agreed. "It's the toys he bought that I can't believe. Have you met any babies lately who can play football?"

"No." She laughed, but she was so nervous about meeting his friends and family that it came out sounding like a croak. At least Brad didn't seem to notice. "Who's your partner now?"

"Wes, until Nick comes back. Wes used to be Katie's partner when they worked vice," he explained.

"You're vice."

"Special vice task force," he corrected.

"I see." There seemed to be a lot of divisions in the police department.

"Then Wes was reassigned to Sylvia for a while."

Cindy nodded again. "It sounds like everybody gets around."

"We try to be flexible." Brad had resumed tossing food into the refrigerator, mindless of whether it needed refrigeration or not.

Cindy sighed to herself. Might as well help Brad prepare the food. Then she'd meet his friends, enjoy the hamburgers, and escape early. "What can I do to help?"

"How are you at preparing kiwi fruit?"

"Almost as good as I am at floors," she said. "And I'm super with strawberries."

"Great." Brad didn't look up, or he might have noticed that she didn't feel as thrilled as she sounded. He was still rummaging through the bags of groceries, looking for the fruit. "Now all we have to do is find them. I should run a dustcloth over the tables, too."

"And a vacuum over the floors," she added.

"You're hired," Brad teased.

They continued to banter back and forth, but throughout their dinner preparations Cindy felt on edge. What would she do when his family and friends came? What if one of his friends recognized and remembered her?

She constantly watched the clock, which ticked so slowly that sometimes it seemed to be going in reverse! Too bad she couldn't speed ahead into a safer time zone.

Nick and Catherine Samuels were the first to arrive. Nick was slightly taller than Brad, and nearly as handsome, but dark, with black hair and blue eyes. Catherine was a pretty blonde. They were opposites, like night and day, and as Cindy had guessed, they were obviously very much in love. Nick showed a heartwarming protectiveness toward Catherine, touching her constantly, and she kept glancing lovingly at him. Because she was well into the advanced stages of pregnancy, she lumbered slightly as she walked.

"Feeling okay, Katie?" Brad asked after he'd introduced Cindy.

"I feel fat, Brad," she answered, smoothing her maternity dress over her protruding abdomen, "but other than that, I'm fine. Ask how Nick is."

Brad laughed. "I don't have to ask that. I already know. He's been driving me crazy."

"Me, too."

"More toys?"

"No, he stopped buying things after the ballet slippers, but I wish you'd get him interested in a case or something so he'd leave me alone. It's nice to have a man around the house, but this one is starting to hover. You'd think I was the only woman in the world ever to have a baby."

"You're the only woman in the world to have *my* baby," Nick said softly, sitting on the arm of the sofa beside her and taking her hand.

Catherine smiled at him, and the look that passed between them was heart-stoppingly beautiful. She turned to Brad and Cindy. "How can I argue with logic like that?"

You couldn't, Cindy thought. For a moment, watching the two of them, sensing the love they shared, she felt like a voyeur. Standing behind her, Brad squeezed her shoulder, as though guessing her thoughts and sharing them.

The doorbell rang before they could say much more. Insisting that she come with him, Brad went to answer it. Soon, more and more people were crowding in, everyone chatting animatedly.

Wes arrived with Sylvia. Brad's new partner was middle-aged, tall, and wiry with thinning red hair and a slight paunch. Sylvia, who Cindy learned had also worked vice with Catherine at one time, sported bright red hair and reminded Cindy of a younger version of Margie, particularly when she spoke.

Sylvia glanced from Brad to Cindy and back again, then smiled, her eyes literally twinkling. "Another one bites the dust, huh? Good thing." She nodded toward Cindy. "She's pretty."

"I know," Brad answered.

"Don't screw up, hotshot." Sylvia turned to Cindy. "Did he tell you he's the most eligible bachelor in the police department and that all the female officers are always chasing after him?"

Cindy didn't doubt it. "No, but he keeps telling me how wonderful he is," she answered, feeling an immediate rapport with the outspoken woman.

"Ignore him," Sylvia advised. "All male cops have big egos. It's the guns they carry. They go around saying, 'My gun is bigger than yours,'" she mocked.

"Hey, Syl," someone called from across the room, "speaking of big guns, where's your date? You're going to be lonesome tonight."

"Nah, I'm like the Marines, honey," she shot back. "I'm looking for a few *good* men."

"I thought you were holding out for a hero," another cop called.

Sylvia waved her hand. "That was last week. Say, big boy," she went on, "how good are you?"

Cindy guessed this kind of banter went on all the time. It was all in fun, and everyone seemed friendly and relaxed. Everyone, that is, except her. The smile on her face felt frozen.

Brad had gone off to the kitchen to check on something, but Wes was still standing beside her. "Confused?" he asked.

"More like overwhelmed," she admitted. Quiet and calm, he conveyed a sense of competence. "There are a lot of people here."

"You'll get to know everybody soon enough."

She doubted that, but appreciated Wes's effort to be friendly and polite, to make her feel accepted. How could she expect him to know about her fears? "Have you been a policeman for a long time?" she asked.

"Do I look that old?"

"Oh, no, you don't look old at all. I'm sorry, I didn't mean it that way."

He flashed another fatherly smile and patted her shoulder. "Don't worry, I know what you meant. I was just teasing you. Actually, I've been on the force for so long that I feel like Methuselah."

"Are you with someone?"

"A date? Not Wes," Sylvia cut in, slipping an arm around the older man's shoulders. "Nobody will have him. Believe it or not, he's looking for an old-fashioned girl—someone to cook and clean for him."

Wes didn't disagree. "The way to a man's heart is through his stomach," he said.

"But in this day and age, my pal," Sylvia said, "a woman's place is not just in the home."

"Is this a private argument?" Brad asked, coming to stand next to Cindy, "or can anyone join in?"

"You're a chauvinist, too," Sylvia said. "I may as well concede the loss now."

"Smart move," Brad said. Just then the doorbell rang again, claiming his attention.

Brad's family arrived in a flurry of smiles, hugs, and greetings. His stepfather, an attractive man, seemed quiet and reserved. Brad's mother and his sister Brenda looked exactly alike, small, pert, and blond. His brother Birk was slightly shorter than Brad, but he also had blond hair and brown eyes. Birk's wife Suzanne and Brenda's husband Mark were open and friendly.

In fact, everyone seemed pleasant—so normal, so suburban. If they only knew, how would they feel about Brad's dating a former stripper? Cindy wondered. Even a former stripper who was now a social worker? The changes she'd made in her life hadn't made any difference to Peter. He'd still condemned her, as had a lot of other men.

But she mustn't keep thinking about those things. Making a conscious effort to put the past out of her mind, Cindy took a sip of her cola. Brad had returned to her side, where his sister Brenda joined them.

Naughty and Nice

Brenda handed Brad a gaily wrapped package. "Aunt Gert sent you a Lady Elizabeth bowl."

"A *real* Lady Elizabeth?" Catherine Samuels asked, overhearing the conversation.

Brenda nodded. "Can you believe it? As if Brad would appreciate antique silver." She sighed and shook her head. "The lengths a family will go for a joke."

Cindy was wondering what she meant when Catherine urged, "Open it Brad. I'll bet it's beautiful."

Brad handed Cindy the package. "Go ahead. You do the honors for me."

Cindy peeled off the ribbon. "What's the family joke?"

"Mother's always lamenting the fact that Brad hasn't found a nice girl and settled down," Brenda said, amusement threading her voice. "Last week Aunt Gert had..." She glanced at Cindy, suddenly looking uncomfortable, as though she was about to commit a social blunder and didn't know how to avoid it.

"Last week Aunt Gert had me to dinner," Brad said, picking up the thread of the conversation. "Along with a friend's daughter, who was an expert on silver."

"That sounds like an interesting evening," Cindy observed, trying to be polite.

"It was," Brad agreed, though she couldn't tell if he was being sarcastic or not.

Cindy opened the package and slipped out the bowl.

"Oh, it *is* lovely." Catherine ran a finger reverently along the rim. "Look at the intricate scrollwork."

"And the gold-washed interior," Brenda added. "That's one of the distinguishing features of a Lady Elizabeth."

The two women went on to discuss the other details that made the bowl a valuable work of art. Although Cindy continued to stand there holding the bowl, she didn't join in the conversation. She knew as much about silver as the man in the moon.

Sylvia and Brad's mother joined them a few minutes

later, and the discussion became more involved. Apparently both women collected silver. Brad left to make someone a drink.

As Cindy listened to the four women talk, she felt even more inadequate. Now it seemed almost funny to recall that at one time she'd thought someday a nice man would want to marry her. Whatever had made her think she could qualify as a suburban housewife? She had taken a gourmet cooking course and a few sewing lessons, but that didn't change what she was, or what she had been. And she'd never, ever be able to discuss antique silver.

The longer the party went on, the more uncomfortable Cindy became. She kept watching Catherine Samuels. Although the pregnant woman was admittedly clumsy, a rosy glow of happiness and contentment surrounded her. A painful emptiness overwhelmed Cindy. It seemed suddenly, achingly obvious that because of her past she would never have the kind of life she wanted—with a husband and a baby to love.

Cindy didn't realize how intently she was staring at Catherine until Brad stood beside her and took her hand. "She's beautiful, isn't she?"

"Yes."

"You know," he added softly, pulling her close, "I just realized that Nick isn't the only fool in the room. If he were me...and she were you...I wouldn't have stopped at buying ballet slippers."

Brad tipped her chin up to kiss her. Cindy felt panic-stricken. What was she going to do? Things were moving too fast. "Brad..." she murmured.

"What?" he whispered back.

But Sylvia popped her head between them. "Oooh! Looks like the party's getting hot. Better watch it, you got a roomful of cops here. Someone's liable to bust you two for lewd and licentious behavior."

Brad laughed and tugged Cindy toward the patio doors.

"Come on," he said, "help me cook the hamburgers so we can feed these people and then get rid of them."

That was easier said than done. The party finally broke up around midnight. Everyone left at about the same time, all hugging Cindy and saying good-bye as though she were a good friend. "See you at the policemen's ball," Sylvia called.

Both Brenda and Brad's mother kissed her on the cheek. "You're a sweet young woman," his mother murmured.

Would she think so if she knew the truth?

Cindy didn't have time to dwell on the woman's remark, because Wes and Sylvia left then, too. Cindy had to say good-bye to them both. And then Catherine and Nick left.

Brad closed the door with a heavy sigh. Cindy yawned and started to gather up ashtrays and dirty dishes, but Brad took them from her and set them back on the table. He tucked her into his arms, snuggling close. "Did you like my friends and family?"

"Yes." Cindy let him hold her; his arms felt wonderfully comfortable. She sighed, resting her head against his chest. "Everyone seemed terrific, though I didn't get to talk with your brother Birk much, or your stepfather. Is your mother divorced from your father?"

"No, my dad died in a railroad accident when I was little. Mom married my stepdad the fall I began high school. Quite a few years ago, actually. They just celebrated their twentieth anniversary."

"How old are you?"

"Thirty-three. An ancient bachelor, according to Mom and my Aunt Gert." He shook his head. "My aunt's a bit strange, but you'd like her."

But would Aunt Gert like Cindy? "Even though she gives you silver bowls?"

"Even though." He paused. "How old are you, Cindy?"

"Twenty-nine."

"You're almost over the hill, too."

She drew back. "Thanks!"

Brad laughed, brushing a lock of hair from her face and tilting her chin up for a quick kiss. "You look tired."

That was an understatement. Cindy felt bleary-eyed. Fatigue had finally caught up with her, and relaxing against him just made it worse. She snuggled deeper, yawning, and said, "I'm having some problems adjusting to your schedule."

"You haven't been able to sleep?"

"Not a lot." She figured she'd had only seven hours of sleep in three days. But he hadn't slept either.

"So much for my seduction plans, but there's always tomorrow. Cindy, why don't you stay here with me tonight? You can have my bed, and I'll bunk on the sofa. Scout's honor."

She smiled, touched by his offer. "Thanks, but I should get home. I shouldn't leave the kittens alone."

"Too bad," he said with a leer.

She gave him a playful whack. "And I thought you meant it about sleeping on the sofa."

Laughing, Brad released her and went to the closet for his shoulder holster and jacket. "I did mean it. Come on, I'll take you home."

"What about the mess?"

"Don't worry, I'll clean it up later."

The car ride was so hypnotic that Cindy almost fell asleep in her seat. At her apartment, Brad prodded her up the stairs and opened the door for her. "Can you manage?"

She paused. "I suppose you'd be glad to help me?"

"Ordinarily I'd be delighted, but I like my women awake when I undress them."

She meant to laugh, but somehow it turned into a yawn instead. A huge one. "I'm sorry, Brad. I'm just so tired."

"Don't worry about it." He kissed her, a chaste peck on the cheek. "Good night, Cindy. Go to bed."

"I will."

She didn't have to be told a second time. She walked into her apartment, fed and watered the cats, pulled on the first nightgown she found, and literally fell into bed, slipping into a deep, delicious sleep.

CHAPTER
Seven

SOMEONE WAS POUNDING on her apartment door.

In her dream Cindy heard loud, frantic knocks, although for some reason she couldn't get to the door. Trying to lift her head, she realized that her doorbell had buzzed, too. How long ago had she become aware of the sounds?

As the woman in her dream floated across the room to answer the door, Cindy turned over, snuggling deeper under the covers. The rapping became sharper. "Cindy! Are you there?" Margie's voice called.

The dream was getting mixed up. Margie hadn't been in it before. Cindy opened her eyes, then closed them. A few seconds later she opened them again and glanced groggily at the clock at her bedside. The digital readout displayed 10:00. Was it morning or night? Since light was streaming in her window, it must be daytime.

"Cindy!" Margie called more sharply. "Cindy, if you're home, will you open the damned door?"

With a start, Cindy realized she wasn't dreaming. Margie was truly pounding on her door. It was ten in the morning, and they were supposed to go shopping.

She forced her eyes open and tossed the blankets aside. Then, with a low, exhausted groan, she fell back down on the bed. Lord, she wished she could sleep forever.

But the pounding on her door continued. She pulled herself upright. "Coming," she called, mixing the word up with a yawn so that it sounded funny.

Margie rattled the knob. "Cindy, are you sick or something? What the hell's going on?"

"Coming!" she called in a louder voice, dragging herself from bed. By now Margie was slapping her palms on the door, trying to shove it open. "Hang on!" Cindy shouted. "I said I was coming!"

"Well, it's about time you answered me!" Margie shouted back. "I figured you had to be home by now."

Cindy stumbled into the living room and opened the door. Margie, who had finally stopped knocking, was standing in the doorway looking irritated. "Well, glory be," she exclaimed as Cindy stood back. "What'd you do, die on the way?"

"I answered, didn't I?"

"Temper, temper, love. Don't be so nasty. You're the one who was rude, not me. I've been standing out here for fifteen minutes getting calluses on my knuckles."

Cindy waved her friend inside. "I forgot this is Saturday."

"First you forget it's Thursday. Now you forget it's Saturday. You're sure having memory lapses these days." Frowning, Margie glanced around the apartment. She looked... suspicious, of all things! "Then you can't get to the door for an hour—"

"You said it took fifteen minutes."

"Whatever, it was a long time."

"I was sleeping."

"Well, at least you're back to normal where that's concerned." She nodded toward Cindy's nightgown. "That looks nice on you. Sexy."

Cindy glanced down at the slinky gown, which Margie had given her for her birthday. "Thanks."

"You're welcome. I'm glad to see you're wearing it." Suddenly Margie smiled, her face lighting up as she glanced toward the bedroom. The door was open, and the bed was disheveled. "I see you had a restless night."

Cindy didn't remember a thing after her head hit the pillow, except her dream this morning. "I guess. I was tired."

"I'll bet. Where were you last evening? I came over, but you weren't home." She leaned forward, craning her neck to peer around the door, trying to see inside the bedroom. Why on earth was she doing that?

"I was out," Cindy said.

"Where?"

"Just out."

"The old guy down the hall said you never came home."

Cindy had always suspected she had nosy neighbors. Margie's remark confirmed it. "Obviously I did come home. I'm here."

"You know what I mean. You didn't come home right after work. And when I called later, you still weren't here." Margie was still craning her neck toward the bedroom. She bent to the floor, presumably to pick up a piece of lint, but Cindy suspected she was trying to see under the bed.

"Looking for something?" she asked.

Margie straightened and grinned. "Yeah, a blind man. I thought maybe you had him in there."

Cindy sighed. Sometimes Margie was too curious for

her own good. "I *told* you, he's not blind."

"Yeah, but is he in there?"

"No, he's not in there."

"Then who were you talking to before?"

"I wasn't talking to anybody. Just you."

"You could have hidden him in the closet."

"I could have shoved him out the window, too."

"You live on the third floor."

"Margie, I didn't hide him anywhere. He's not here."

"Were you out with him last night?"

Secrets. Suddenly she had so many of them—from Brad, from Margie. She wondered if she was the only one being fooled. "Look, this is silly," she said. "I'm sorry I slept so soundly and that you had to knock for so long. As soon as I feed the cats, I'll get dressed so we can go shopping. Do you want to go downtown?"

"Oh, I forgot," Margie said. "I came to tell you I can't go shopping today."

Cindy paused, exasperated. "You came all the way over here and woke me up to tell me you can't go shopping today?"

"Is something wrong with that?" Margie looked offended.

"Yes, something's wrong with that," Cindy said. "I was asleep."

"Jeez, I'm sorry." The redhead huffed as though she'd been mortally wounded. "You don't have to attack me."

"You're right." Cindy sighed. "I didn't mean to snap. I'm just so tired these days."

"Maybe you'd better go for a checkup."

"That's not a bad idea." Maybe she *should* go for a checkup, Cindy thought. Between the turmoil Brad Jordan had caused in her and her lack of sleep, she was so confused it was a miracle she knew her own name.

"Look, I've got to run," Margie said. "Don't forget we have tickets for the fashion show Monday night."

"I won't."

Margie started to leave, then took one last look around, glancing toward the kitchen.

"Will you stop this nonsense?" Cindy demanded. "I told you there's no one here!"

"Just checking. By the way." Margie paused at the door. "Where are those laundry baskets I gave you?"

The kittens were asleep, all curled up on the sofa, oblivious of what was going on around them. Sam was lying on a cushion cleaning herself. "In the closet," Cindy answered. "Why?"

Margie nodded toward the window just before she left. "Looks like you ought to start using them." She waved good-bye and left the apartment.

Turning, Cindy was horrified at what she saw: Below the window and all along the bottom near the baseboard bits of wallpaper had been ripped into strips and hung off the wall.

"Oh, no!" She rushed to examine the damage. Damn! She didn't have any wallpaper left. She'd used every bit of it when she'd originally papered the room! She'd have to glue the strips in place and hope the drapes, when they were in place, would hide the mess. "Bad kitties!" she said, but of course the felines were all sound asleep and didn't hear her. She sighed and got out a bottle of glue.

After she'd repaired the wall as best as she could, Cindy went to call the veterinarian. Perhaps Dr. Wallace could suggest a more effective way of training the kittens than squirting water on them. The telephone rang before she could pick it up.

"Cindy?" It was Brad. "Morning, babe. Did you sleep well?"

Even over the phone his voice sounded sexy. Cindy felt a tender surge of emotion. Why was he so devastating to her senses? She didn't even mind that he called her "babe." In fact, on his lips the word sounded like an endearment. "I slept fine," she said, "but I could use another fifty hours."

He chuckled. "That tired, huh? Listen, I can't talk long. I'm at the station house."

"I thought you had the day off." She glanced at her watch. It was just past ten.

"Something came up late last night that I had to take care of. But I just realized I have a lot of leftovers from the barbecue. I think I'll be finished here by five. Since this is technically still my day off, how about if I pick you up and we have another cookout?"

"Have you already called everybody else?"

"I wasn't planning to invite anyone but you."

Oh. Obviously that meant they'd be alone. At the prospect, her heart started beating frantically. "No friends or family?" she asked.

"Just you and me. What do you think?"

She thought it was great. She also thought it was dangerous. But before she could answer, someone called to him in the background.

"Hold on a second," he said. Cindy could hear him talking to the person in low mumbles. When he got back to her, he was in a hurry. "I've got to run, babe. See you at five."

The line went dead. Cindy stood for a moment still holding the receiver. She should call him back and say no, but she didn't. So much for heeding the danger warnings.

Sighing, she hung up and flipped open her address book to search for Dr. Wallace's number, only to run across Rebecca Wade's number instead.

Of all the women with whom Cindy had worked at Club Arnaud, Rebecca had been the first to whom her past hadn't mattered. In fact, Rebecca was now married to the state's attorney for the city of Chicago. In a way it was ironic. A former exotic dancer and a lawyer who held one of the highest law-enforcement positions in the city had married and were living happily ever after.

It had been a long time since Cindy had talked to her friend—too long. Would Rebecca be home? The last thing she should do today was go visiting. She should get some rest. She should call the vet. She *had* to do something about Brad Jordan. But instead of doing any of those things, she dialed her friend's number.

Rebecca sounded delighted to hear from her, and immediately invited her over. She and Steven lived fairly nearby, on the near North side in a large, comfortable town house. Cindy took the bus. When she arrived, Rebecca answered the door with a dish towel in her hands.

"Cindy! How are you?" Rebecca hugged her. "Come on in!"

"You always look so great, Becky," Cindy said. Rebecca still had dark, waist-length hair and, despite having delivered two children, she had managed to maintain her slim shape. "I see a couple streaks of gray, though," Cindy teased.

"I earned those gray hairs," Rebecca declared. "Every one of them. Don't forget, I have two teenagers."

Cindy smiled. Shawn, Steven's son from a previous marriage, and Danny, Rebecca's son from her first marriage, had both recently turned fourteen. "That bad, huh?"

Rebecca shook her head. "Not really. The boys are good, just full of energy. They're out back with Steven now, playing basketball. Shall I call them? They'll be glad to see you."

"Let them play for a while," Cindy said. "I'll catch them later." She glanced into the living room, hoping to see their daughter, a pert six-year-old who was an exact replica of her mother. "Where's Jenny?"

"Next door playing with a friend. She'll be home in

a bit. I'm baking cookies, so I know she'll show up at any moment." Rebecca laughed. "They'll *all* show up at any moment."

"They can smell the cookies from outside?"

"Yes, it's like a homing device." They walked into the kitchen. The sink was full of dirty dishes, and cookie trays, containing both baked and unbaked cookies, covered the counters. "Come on, you can lick the bowl before Steven comes in and finds it. He's going to develop a paunch if I don't watch him."

Cindy laughed. Paunch or not, Steven Wade was, and would remain, one of the most handsome men she'd ever known. She doubted Rebecca minded either. They'd been married for almost eight years now and still acted like honeymooners.

"I'm glad you stopped by," Rebecca said when Cindy had perched on a stool in the midst of the mess. "Margie tells me you've been upset lately."

Cindy glanced up sharply. She should have known Rebecca would come straight to the point. And she should have known Margie had already blabbed. "Margie's talked to you about me?"

"She's been concerned about you," Rebecca said. "I am, too. Is everything all right?"

All at once Cindy realized she needed to talk to someone. Perhaps unconsciously that's why she'd come. She had to tell somebody about Brad Jordan. Maybe she should have spoken to Margie, but, despite their being best friends, their views on men were very different. Margie figured "love 'em and leave 'em" was the only philosophy that made sense. In the past, when she'd sown her wild oats, Cindy had felt that way herself. But since she'd matured, since she'd changed, she'd wanted more than casual sex from relationships.

Truthfully, though, she hadn't confided in Margie because she had been avoiding the issue. She was too busy to think, or too tired, or too something. The result was that she'd continually put off facing her dilemma. It was about time she confronted the fact that all the while she'd been telling herself nothing was going to happen between herself and Brad Jordan, something *had* happened. It *was* happening. And she didn't know what to do about it.

"No," she finally told Rebecca, "everything isn't all right. In fact, everything's awful."

Rebecca paused in dropping batter onto a cookie sheet, standing with her hand poised in midair. "What's the problem?"

"At the risk of sounding trite, what's always the problem with women? Men. I've met somebody."

Rebecca dropped the spoon and sat down across from Cindy, her expression serious. "But that's wonderful."

"No, it isn't," Cindy said softly. "Or at least at the moment it doesn't seem so great." She sighed. "Becky, how do you know when you're in love?"

"That"s a difficult question to answer," Rebecca said. "Different people feel different things. All I can share is my own personal experience. I knew I loved Steven when caring for his needs became more important than caring for my own."

"That's not quite what I need to know," Cindy finally admitted. "I want to know, how do you know when someone is in love with you?"

"That's an even harder question to answer," Rebecca said. "But I don't think you're looking for the answer to that question, either. I think you want the assurance that you're not going to get hurt, right?"

It was all too true. Cindy took a deep breath. "Becky, I haven't told him."

"About your past?" Rebecca asked gently.

Cindy nodded. "I should have told him right away. I should have told Peter right away, too. I've made so many mistakes in my life. Becky, I don't know if I *can* tell him... ever. I'm so afraid of being hurt again."

"Because of Peter?"

"He hurt me the most. I hurt him, too. He was so devastated that night. I don't think I'll ever forget the expression on his face. I guess I'm only fooling myself. No matter how many times I tell myself that my past doesn't matter, I know it does matter and that I'll never live it down."

"Cindy, one day your past *won't* matter. This may be hard to believe, but one day you'll meet a great guy who will understand. He won't care about the things you did years ago."

"I wish that were true."

"It is. Peter was a nice guy, but he didn't love you. He couldn't have and still have hurt you like that. You are one of the most terrific people I know, Cindy Marshall," Rebecca went on firmly, "and someday you'll make a great wife and mother."

"You say that because you know me."

"And the man you're dating knows you too—or he soon will," Rebecca pointed out. "What's he like?"

"Brad?" Cindy shrugged. "He's nice."

"That's all?"

"Well, he's handsome and fun and kind and tender and loving and understanding and wonderful and—" She shrugged again. "I don't know what else to say about him, except that he's special." And she wanted so much for things to work out between them.

"If this guy's anything like the man you just described," Rebecca said, "tender, loving, and understanding, then no matter what he finds out about you, he won't reject you as Peter and the others did."

The oven timer buzzed. Rebecca got up to turn it off and took a tray of cookies from the oven. "Maybe you're not sure Brad's the man you think he is."

"I'm sure he's special." Cindy gave a half-laugh. "Did I tell you he's a cop?"

Rebecca paused with another cookie tray half inside the oven. "You're dating a policeman?" she asked incredulously.

Cindy waved her hand. "You don't have to say it, I know it's unbelievable. There are two people in this world who would never date a policeman—me and Margie. But guess what? I'm dating a policeman. Oh, Becky, what am I going to do?"

"Take a chance."

Cindy glanced up sharply. "What?"

"Sometimes you have to take a chance on love," Rebecca explained. "If you don't, you'll never know if it could work or not."

Cindy thought about that for a moment. "What about being hurt?"

Rebecca set the cookies on top of the stove. "What about it? Cindy, there aren't any guarantees in life."

Cindy sighed. How true.

"I'm sorry," Rebecca suddenly exclaimed. "I've been a terrible hostess. How about some coffee? Would you like a cookie?"

"No, thanks." Cindy patted her thighs. "I have to watch my own weight, and I'd better get going, anyhow. The kittens are loose. Just this morning they tore down part of the wallpaper."

"Pets can be as much of a pain as love can be." Rebecca laughed. "And believe me, I know."

Cindy laughed, too. Rebecca and Steven's children owned an entire menagerie of pets: a cat, a bird, tropical fish, several guinea pigs, a snake, a tarantula, and just recently Jennifer had acquired an ant farm. "I guess I'm glad I have just the kittens," Cindy said. "I might have come across a pregnant, abandoned ant last year and adopted it!"

"Or a spider. Don't worry, the kittens *will* eventually outgrow their mischievousness."

"I hope so."

"And, Cindy," Rebecca added, hugging her, "I know things will work out for you. Good luck, hon."

"Thanks, Becky. Oh, how's Monica?" Rebecca's sister was a famous model in New York City.

"Doing great. She just signed a contract to be the new Chambers girl. Perfume ads will never be the same."

"At least she's come a long way from modeling pantyhose," Cindy said, laughing.

When she got home, Cindy realized she had forgotten to mention to Rebecca that she'd heard Tony had sold Club Arnaud. She hadn't told Margie, either, but it was too late to call them. Brad would be here to pick her up in less than an hour.

Thank goodness the kittens hadn't done any more damage. Cindy fed them and headed for the shower. She still hadn't decided what to do about Brad, but after talking with Rebecca, she was eager to have dinner with him. Perhaps tonight she would get up the courage to tell him about her past. She had to do it soon. She couldn't keep putting off the inevitable.

Brad arrived at the stroke of five. Cindy was surprised at how tired he looked. He was handsome, all right, and as sexy as ever, but lines of fatigue stood out around his eyes.

"Did you work all night?" she asked.

He nodded. "All day, too."

"Tough case?"

"Very tough. We've got a major drug bust going down."

"Don't you have to be there now?"

"Not yet. These things take time. If the station needs me, they have both our phone numbers."

"Are you sure you still want to have dinner? I'll understand if you want to go home and sleep."

Brad laughed. "I think you just want to sleep yourself, Cindy Marshall. For another fifty hours, I think you said. Anyway," he added with a wicked grin, "if I feel miserable tonight, you can comfort me."

"I can just imagine what kind of comfort you have in mind, Brad Jordan," she teased.

"A sweet guy like me? Cindy, shame on you." He laughed again. "Ready?"

Cindy knew she should stay home. He was stealing her heart, and she didn't have the strength to cry for help. But she grabbed her sweater and turned to Sam. "Look, you're going to have to start watching your kittens. No more wallpaper chewing."

"What'd they do?" Brad asked.

"That." She gestured to her wall.

"Little devils, aren't they?" he said as they left her apartment.

The day was still bright and sunny. Cindy wore slacks and a loose silken top. As usual, Brad slipped on his sunglasses.

"Why do you wear those?" she asked.

He glanced at her and shrugged. "To ward off the sun's harmful rays."

"You wear them on cloudy days, too."

"Would you believe I want to look macho?"

"You're macho, all right, but those sunglasses almost seem to be a symbol for you."

"I guess they are," he agreed, lifting them off and looking at them. He paused for the briefest moment. "You've heard the expression, 'Viewing life through rose-colored glasses'? Well, I guess I'm viewing life through mirrored lenses."

She didn't quite follow what he was saying. "So that some of life's harshness gets reflected back out to the world, instead of absorbed by you?"

"Maybe." He looked thoughtful for a moment. "I guess. In my line of work, I see a lot of awful things. Speaking of which," he added, his tone lightening, "I hired a Swedish maid today."

Obviously he felt uncomfortable talking about himself and his painful experiences as a policeman. She could imagine just how awful the things he saw were. "Is she a blonde?" she asked, picking up on his change of subject.

"Yes, but unfortunately she's also about my mother's age."

They had reached his car. As Cindy slid into the seat, she glanced over her shoulder at the bags lined up on the back seat. "What are the groceries for?"

"Dinner. Didn't I tell you I thought we'd barbecue again?"

"You said you had leftovers."

He got in on his side. "I needed some more chili sauce."

If the number of bags was any indication, he'd bought out the entire store again. "How many jars did you buy?"

Smiling, he started the engine and pulled into the flow of traffic. "Only three or four. I got some more kiwi fruit, too. You can make another fruit salad."

"The same menu two nights in a row? I thought you could cook, Brad Jordan."

"Hey! Is that an insult?"

"Yes."

"Okay, Cindy Marshall, tomorrow *you* can cook dinner."

She laughed.

When they arrived at his apartment, Brad handed her a bag to carry. This time his apartment was immaculate, including the kitchen. The Swedish maid had done a good job.

Brad fixed the hamburgers and they went out onto the terrace, which was nearly as large as his one-room apartment, and decorated just as nicely. Last night there had been so many people, and it had been so dark out, Cindy hadn't looked around much. Now, as he started the charcoal fire, she noticed the wrought-iron patio furniture tastefully arranged around pots of flowers. Evidently Brad either spent a great deal of time here on the terrace or paid somebody to maintain his plants, which were green and thick.

"Do you like petunias?" he asked.

"Yes, I do, but I was admiring your asparagus plant. It's growing very nicely."

"Is that what the green stuff's called? I never knew what it was. A clerk in the garden store sold it to me."

"Did you buy it on impulse," she asked, "or because the clerk was a cute chick?"

"Cindy! You've wounded me to the quick. I bought it on impulse, of course." He opened a can of chili sauce and placed it over the coals to heat.

"Is *that* your secret hot sauce?" she exclaimed, pretending to be horrified.

"Oops! Caught in the act."

"It's a good thing you don't live in Texas, Brad Jordan. The natives would run you out of town."

"Mustn't tell, now. You'll ruin my reputation."

"Good," she bantered back. "It deserves to be ruined."

"You know," he drawled, "that mean streak of yours is getting wider."

"But I'm so sweet," she objected.

While he cooked dinner, they chatted about whether mustard or ketchup tasted better on hamburgers, whether the Chicago Cubs would finish the season in first place, whether plants liked rainwater better than tap water. Finally he handed her a juicy hamburger on a bun and a fruit salad.

"Dinner is served, madam," he said with a bow and a sweep of his hand.

"Looks good." Cindy settled in a comfortable chair to enjoy her meal. In a few moments Brad joined her, choosing a chaise longue next to her. Under his arm he carried a bottle of red Beaujolais. He removed the cork and poured two glasses.

"Since you liked the sunrise the other morning," he said, handing her a glass, "you should enjoy the sunset. I have a really good view of it out here."

Cindy glanced toward the west. The sun did hang low in the sky, but it wasn't quite sunset yet. "This is a beautiful terrace. You must really enjoy it."

"I do. When I'm home."

"Your job requires long hours, doesn't it?"

"Yes, but I work even more than I have to." He shrugged. "One thing about being a cop, or at least a detective, is that you can bury yourself in the job. You can live with reality twenty-four hours a day, if you want to."

"Do you want to do that?"

"I did." His gaze held hers. "Until recently."

The words were soft and not at all what she'd expected him to say, and she wasn't certain exactly what he meant. Until recently? Until he met her? She began to say something, but he had reached for the wine bottle.

"More?" he asked.

"Please."

"How about another hamburger?"

"Okay," she said, telling herself there was nothing to be nervous about. It wasn't as though he'd made a declaration of eternal love. She wasn't even certain what his intense gaze and casual comment, *until recently,* had actually meant. Besides, she didn't want to think about it. She didn't want to confront what she knew was happening between them.

Cindy hadn't realized how hungry she was. She ate a second hamburger and drank another glass of wine. By the time they were finished, she felt not only stuffed, but deliciously tired. She leaned back in her chair.

"Oh, look," she said, suddenly noticing the sunset. Brilliant red and gold streaks filled the sky. She got up and went to the other end of the terrace where there was a better view. "It's beautiful."

Walking up behind her, Brad slid his arms around her waist and pulled her back until she was leaning against him, her head on his shoulder. The embrace was so natural, it felt so comfortable, that she didn't think to object.

"Very beautiful," he said, running a hand up and down her arm. She sensed at once that he wasn't talking about the sunset. She shivered but didn't move away.

"Cold?" he asked.

"No."

"Good." He cuddled her tighter, nodding toward the sun. When he spoke, his breath was soft against her ear. "Look at that red. It's so vibrant. Did you know the colors are produced by the refraction of the sun's rays through water? The dispersing action of millions of tiny water droplets in the path of sunlight makes up what's called a solar spectrum."

"My." Cindy was impressed. She'd never thought much about light rays and the sunset, and she was having trouble maintaining her composure. "Did you study meteorology in school?"

"Some. Actually I learned that theory from a loonie I arrested. He kept raving about the solar spectra, wanting me to understand how complex something as simple as the sunset could be to scientists. I found out later that he was a professor of astronomy at one of the big universities here."

"Why did you arrest him?"

"For being a public nuisance. He kept waylaying people and forcing them to listen to his dire predictions."

"Poor guy."

"I think the pressure got to him, and he just cracked," Brad explained. "Whenever I watch a sunset now, I think of him and the solar spectra." He pulled her a tad closer. Instinctively she snuggled against him. "Makes me sound smart, too. Something with which to impress the ladies."

She smiled. She could imagine how he impressed the ladies. "Shame on you, Brad Jordan."

"Why? They love it."

"I'm sure they do, but what if it's not true? Did you check out the theory?"

"No. True or not, it sounds good. It sure impressed the old lady at the grocery store."

"I think she impressed you more. You bought all those groceries. And for some reason I think it's the younger ladies you should be trying to impress," she teased, "not the older ones."

Brad paused for the longest moment. Finally he said huskily, "There's only one woman I want to impress, Cindy, and that's you."

The sunset had given way to twilight. Scattered stars shimmered in the sky. Cindy wasn't certain when Brad had turned her so that she was facing him, but suddenly she realized she was molded against him, looking up at him. His arms held her in a protective circle, one around her waist, the other softly caressing her back.

All at once she realized that soft music had started to play and that the patio glowed with low, incandescent lights. Apparently Brad had thought of everything when outfitting his apartment.

"And I do want to impress you," he added in a low whisper.

Cindy shivered as his breath blew softly around her ear and curled along the slope of her neck. She waited for him to kiss her. His lips brushed hers lightly. "Nice."

Now. She had to tell him now. "Brad..."

She tried to pull back, but he had started to move across the patio in a slow waltz step. "You know, we never did get around to those dance lesson," he whispered in her ear. "How about a quick one now? The music's nice."

The music *was* nice, a soft Gershwin tune. Cindy licked her lips nervously. "I'm not a very good dance instructor." Aside from a few traditional steps, all she knew how to do was strip.

He pulled her closer. "You don't have to be good to teach me the basics, do you?"

"I guess not." She was becoming a champion at putting things off. Besides, he was holding her so tightly. She moved his hand from her waist, taking it in her own. "Your hand goes here."

"It feels more natural here," he said, encircling her waist again with both his hands.

"It isn't right, though."

"It'll be fine. Put your arms around my neck."

Cindy hadn't the will to object. She did as he'd suggested, brushing her hands lightly through his thick blond hair, acutely aware of the hard length of his body as she pressed against him.

"What do we do now?" he asked.

"For a simple waltz you just move in a square."

"Like this?" He moved sideways, then forward, then sideways, and back again, in a perfect box.

"Yes," she said.

"But shouldn't we be closer?" He wrapped his hands tighter around her waist.

"A bit." Her voice caught in her throat as her thighs brushed against his. "I think that's too close."

"It feels comfortable, Cindy. Natural."

Too comfortable, Cindy thought, and much too natural.

Holding her securely, Brad started to move to the beat

of the music, slowly forward and across, back and over. She followed his lead without question, letting her body meld into his. Sensations clamored inside her, and sharp, poignant longing.

"Cindy?" he whispered.

"Yes?"

"Am I doing okay?"

More than okay. "Yes," she murmured.

"I think I've got it."

She thought he did, too, particularly when his lips descended to hers. The kiss was all that she expected it to be—tender, yet demanding; soft, but at the same time firm. With a low groan, he gathered her so close that she could feel the need in him, and she arched against him as his lips moved over hers, brushing, stroking, evoking sensations she never knew existed. In her mind she saw soft, delicate rose petals flutter to the ground to form a velvet bed of eternal love. She smelled the fragrance, sweet and slightly flowery.

Suddenly Cindy knew that she was in over her head. She was having delusions. She tried to pull away. "Brad..."

But he held her gently captured in his embrace. "Cindy, don't be afraid," he murmured huskily. "I won't hurt you, love. Please don't turn away from me. We've come too far."

There was so much he didn't know. Lord, she had to tell him! She had to say it! Tears sprang to her eyes. "Brad—"

"Don't talk, Cindy," he murmured. "Not now, not when I need you. I need you so much, babe, and we've waited so long."

She needed him, too. Oh, how she needed him! She swallowed the tears that had sprung to her eyes. What would one evening hurt? One evening of love. One evening of gathering rose petals.

Sometimes you have to take a chance.

Oh, Lord, could she? Should she? She was so torn. Didn't she deserve something? Just one special moment with the man she loved? And she did love Brad Jordan, though they hadn't known each other very long. Without a doubt she loved him.

She hesitated for the longest time, but finally she whispered, "I want to be close to you. As close as it's possible to be."

"Cindy?"

She continued to meet his gaze, allowing her love to shine in her eyes. "Yes, Brad?"

"Oh, Cindy." In one lithe movement he swept her into his arms and carried her inside and behind the screen to lay her gently on his bed. "I need you. Cindy, I need you so much."

CHAPTER
Eight

A SMALL LAMP glowed on the table beside them. Brad undressed Cindy by its light, taking her clothes off item by item, slowly, with exquisite care. First her blouse, undoing the buttons carefully, as though each were a precious stone that he might crush between his fingertips. Brushing the garment aside, he peeled it from her shoulders and tossed it to the foot of the bed in a silky pool. Her bra was of a beige lace that contrasted with the creamy white of her skin. Trailing one finger lightly across to where the tops of her breasts peeked tantalizingly, he unhooked the snap, allowing the creamy mounds to spring forth proud and free. She lay on the bed below him in the semidarkness, her senses coming alive as he removed the rest of her clothes, touched by the awe in his eyes as he saw her naked for the very first time.

"Oh, Cindy, you're beautiful," he murmured, "so very beautiful."

Gently he touched her breasts, cupping the fullness with his palms, first one, then the other. Then he leaned down to kiss them, brushing his lips lightly back and forth across her feverish skin.

Cindy felt inflamed by his touch. "Brad," she whispered.

He didn't allow her to say more. Gathering her close, he kissed her lips as softly and gently as he had touched her breasts. One hand slid across her stomach in a slow caress. Chills traversed her body while her skin burned with a feverish warmth.

When his hand paused at the apex of her legs, she held her breath until at last he slipped his fingers gently into her warmth. She gasped with pleasure as he began a slow rhythmic movement that set her on fire. Moaning, she arched higher, seeking the erotic promise of his quest.

"Oh, Brad," she breathed softly.

His tongue slid inside her mouth, entwining with hers. Cindy opened herself to him, curling her hands around his neck to pull him even closer. As he continued a rhythmic caress with his hand, he moved his lips down her breast to gently take her nipple into his mouth. Cindy saw a cluster of stars, all the suns in the universe spinning around and around as he trailed a torrid brand across her skin with his lips, down, down, to the core of her being. Then the stars exploded one by one, giant fireballs, red and green and gold and silver. Sparks flew through the sky in a burst of color.

"Oh, Brad," she moaned again, not knowing why, yet compelled to say his name.

"Tell me, love. Tell me what you feel." He slid up her body to pause beside her, gazing tenderly down at her.

Their eyes held, but she felt so overwhelmed with emotion, with love, that she couldn't speak. Without conscious thought of what she was doing, she reached for him, trailing her hand inside his shirt, along his chest, over his shoulder, down his arm as far as his clothing would allow. She wanted to touch him as he had touched her, to pleasure him as he had just pleasured her.

"Wait." He paused and slipped off his shirt. Just as quickly he shed the rest of his clothing. He pulled his briefs down over his hips and stood for a moment, outlined in the candlelight.

Perhaps *beautiful* wasn't an apt description for a man, but at that moment, to Cindy, Brad Jordan was beautiful, his golden, sculpted body strong, powerful, and magnificent.

She reached out to him once more. He hesitated a moment, poised beside her. "Cindy, are you sure this is what you want?" he asked softly, and his expression was so sincere that she wanted to cry.

"Yes," she whispered. "This is what I want."

Still he didn't move. "Tell me, Cindy," he whispered. "Tell me you want me."

She could stop. She could get dressed and go home right now; he was giving her the chance to change her mind.

"I want you," she said simply.

"No, love, you have to say it. You have to tell me, out loud, what you want. I have to know this is a conscious decision for you."

She looked directly at him. "I want you to make love with me, Brad."

"You won't feel any regret?"

Cindy regretted many things about her past, and she knew she would make mistakes in the the future. But she would never regret this moment with Brad.

She closed her eyes to prevent tears from streaming down her face as she shook her head. "No, I won't feel any regret."

"Look at me," he said.

She opened her eyes.

"You're beautiful, Cindy Marshall. The most beautiful woman I've ever known, and I want you, too." Reaching out with one hand, he caressed her face, tenderly brushing away the teardrop that had fallen to her cheek. "But I can't make love with you if you cry. It wouldn't be right."

"I won't cry."

"Sure?"

"I'm sure." Taking his hand, she drew it to her breast.

Brad caressed her softly, tenderly. The moment stretched into an eternity as he knelt beside her, then leaned closer and closer, inch by torturous inch, until at last, their mouths met in a brief, tender kiss.

"Cindy. Oh, Cindy," he murmured against her lips.

Finally, giving in to his emotions, he clutched her to him with a husky groan, his lips moving commandingly over hers, with an intensity that was at once exhilarating and frightening. She was crushed against him, body to body, flesh to flesh. In a maze of arms and legs, they lay on the bed.

Though his lips were rough, Brad stroked her body gently. Cindy felt ablaze with the fiery sensations of his caresses; everywhere he touched, tiny flames licked at her skin, scorching her. A white-hot longing raged through her until she arched against him. All she could think of was the feel of him next to her, the texture of his skin, the hairs that prickled sensuously along her legs and thighs as he pressed his body tightly to hers.

"Oh, love," he said, his voice thick as he trailed his mouth across her breasts.

It wasn't a question, but Cindy knew that he was asking. "Yes," she murmured back. "Now, Brad, Love me now."

He whispered her name again, nudging her thighs apart and arching above her.

Time stood still as he waited; then in one swift movement he made them one. He gave a half-gasp of pleasure, then began to move in an age-old rhythm. "Oh, Cindy, you're mine," he murmured hoarsely. "I can't believe you're mine."

The sensations that had left her breathless before paled in comparison to the feelings that blazed through her now. As Brad moved inside her, brilliant meteors exploded and flared across the sky in a holocaust of light, until she thought surely she would die from the intensity of her need. She tossed her head from side to side and clutched him closer. Finally, just when she thought she could stand no more, pleasure spread through her in giant tremors, and she gasped with wild, sweet release.

"Oh, Brad," she gasped.

He clutched her tighter as the same tremors racked his body. "Cindy!"

And then he lay still on top of her.

Afterward, neither of them moved for many minutes. Cindy's heart pounded furiously in her chest, and she could feel Brad's breath coming hot and hard against her throat, where his head lay in the curve of her neck.

When she lived in the Southwest she'd heard that certain Indian tribes believed that when a man climaxed, he gave his woman the ultimate gift, a part of his soul, and that was why he was weak for a while afterward. At the time she'd been too young to appreciate the beauty of the belief, but now she understood. She felt as if she had just been given Brad's soul. Awed by their union, she stroked his hair lovingly.

He shifted position, taking his weight from her body yet still holding her close. He brushed her hair back from her sweat-dampened face, his touch as soft as a petal. "No regrets?" he asked softly.

She shook her head. "None."

"You know you're beautiful."

"Yes," she murmured, "you told me that a lot."

"I mean it," he said. "You're a very beautiful woman."

He made her feel that way. She touched his cheek reverently. "Thank you, Brad."

"For what?"

"For... for giving me a part of you."

"Was it good for you?"

"Yes." She'd never felt this way before, so overwhelmed with love. "Yes, it was wonderful."

"I'm glad." He tweaked her nose. "But we'd better cut the mushy stuff. I'll get a swelled head. Don't forget the size of my ego."

"Giant." She laughed and then, sighing contentedly, snuggled her cheek against his chest.

"Thirsty?" He nuzzled her forehead with his lips. "Want something to drink?"

She was content to be near him. "No. What's the matter? Are you restless?"

"Just trying to be a good host."

A good host! After what they'd just shared? "Oh, thanks!" she said, lifting her head to glare at him with mock anger.

Looking around now, she noticed this area of the room for the first time. What appeared to be a gilt bird cage decorated a corner, and mirrors covered one entire wall. There were satin sheets on the bed, as she'd once imagined, but they were beige, not black, and the single light that glowed on the bedside table was in the shape of a candle. Soft, romantic music from the stereo filled the room.

Brad Jordan's bedroom *was* a regular den of iniquity! Cindy couldn't keep from staring into the mirror. She could see their reflections clearly, and the vision was strangely erotic. He'd tossed a leg casually over hers, and his hand on her hip absently caressed her. His darker skin contrasted with her paler body and . . . and she felt herself flush with erotic need just from looking at them.

"I like your bedroom," she said, trailing a hand along the bed. "The sheets are sensuous."

"Thanks."

"Where they your decorator's idea or yours?"

She sensed his grin. "Cindy, do you think I'd let a decorator choose my sheets?"

"Come on, 'fess up. Which? You or your lady decorator?"

"How do you know she was a lady?"

"I can tell. Whose idea were the sheets?"

"Mine," he said with a chuckle. "Cindy, I had to do *some* things myself, and my bedroom is my domain."

"You have terrific taste, Brad Jordan." She laughed and nodded toward the cage. She could see a bird inside, sitting on a perch. It looked like a fake bird, but a box of real seeds underneath suggested that it was alive and waiting to be fed. "Is your decorator responsible for that, too?"

"No, Katie gave me Tweety. She said I needed something to worry about."

"And do you worry about it?"

He laughed. "Cindy, it's a fake bird."

She laughed, too, then turned serious. "Brad, what made you become a cop?"

He shrugged. "I don't know for sure." They were still lying together, their legs entwined. "A lot of things, I guess. I think I really decided the day I came back to Chicago to visit some old buddies, and I saw the girl I had been in love with in eighth grade standing on a corner soliciting for prostitution. It was a cold, snowy day, and she wasn't even wearing a coat.

"Quite a few girls in my neighborhood had supported themselves that way, so I didn't think too much about it until her pimp pulled to the curb in his Cadillac Coupe

DeVille, wearing a beaver coat, and started slapping her face because she hadn't earned enough money. I hadn't seen that girl in several years, but when we were kids I really cared for her, and right then I wanted to kill the guy. Later that night I figured, no, let's do it legally and put him away forever. I applied for the police academy the next morning."

Obviously he was describing a very rough neighborhood. Cindy was stunned to realize that she and Brad had grown up in the same kind of environment. "I thought you were from the suburbs," she said.

"I am," he answered, "but I grew up in Chicago. I thought I told you we moved to Downers Grove when I went into high school. That's when my mother married my stepfather."

"Did you ever arrest the pimp?"

Brad nodded. "It took me a long time. Fifteen years, in fact, but I finally got him. He's in Marion State Penitentiary, for good, I hope."

"What about the girl?"

"I lost track of Lisa. A couple of months after I saw her that day, she packed up and ran out on the jerk. I like to think she made it, that she ended up married to a nice guy, with a couple kids."

They both knew the story seldom ended so happily. Teenage runaways, particularly girls, were a target for every degenerate known to mankind. Cindy ought to know. Yet she'd been lucky; she'd found Club Arnaud, Rebecca, Margie, and all the other people who had helped her. But only after a long, frightening journey during which she'd tried almost everything.

"Anyhow, wherever Lisa is, I got the bastard for her," Brad went on. "What about you? What made you become a social worker?"

She should tell him now. Here was another perfect opportunity. But all she could say was, "I drifted into it.

I took some courses and discovered I like counseling, and I know how kids think." She gave a half-laugh. "I used to think that way myself."

"Sounds as if you have good qualifications."

She shrugged. *Brad, I used to do those bad things myself.*

Nine simple words, but they wouldn't come. Cindy's stomach was churning with so many conflicting emotions, she didn't know what to say or do. *Tell him!* her mind screamed.

"What time is it?" Brad glanced at the clock. "You know, we never gave your kittens that caviar I bought. Maybe we should go check on them now."

"What made you think of that?" Cindy asked. Whatever it was, she was grateful. She'd been given another reprieve.

"The bird." He got out of bed and pulled on his pants. "Do you remember where I put the cans?"

She got up too. "Check the refrigerator. But maybe we should skip the caviar. I don't like to spoil the cats. They can be so finicky."

"Cindy," Brad said, "everybody needs to spoil pets. That's what they're for."

Brad brought along the caviar. When they arrived at her apartment, he insisted on opening all five cans so that each cat could have its own treat. "Can't leave anybody out," he said, placing the bowls in a row on the floor. "Sibling rivalry, you know."

"Cats don't experience sibling rivalry," she corrected, watching the animals scurry to their bowls. "Children do."

"I hear they're easily spoiled, too. Do you like kids, Cindy? Other than teenagers," he quickly amended.

"Yes, I like kids."

"Good. I do, too. You know, Cindy, I don't have any cats."

She frowned. "I know. And . . . ?"

"And that means I'm all alone."

He pushed away from the counter and started toward her, his stance aggressive, all authoritative male. "I don't have any pets. I don't have any attachments," he went on, his gaze never leaving her face as he slowly approached her. "I don't have anybody to feed. I don't have anybody to hurry home to. And right now it's very late."

Now she knew exactly what he was getting at. "Yes, it is," she answered. "Very late indeed."

"And it's a long way home."

Actually he lived only a few miles away, but sometimes distance was relative. She nodded in agreement. "It is."

"And I'm awfully tired."

"So you'd like to stay here for the night."

"Right. Do you suppose these little critters will be content now and go to sleep?" He indicated the kittens, who were fastidiously cleaning their paws.

"No. Cats are nocturnal creatures. They'll be up all night. But we could close the bedroom door."

"Good thinking," he said. "I'll race you to the bedroom. The loser has to get the ice packs."

"The loser gets the *what?*" she asked, hoping he didn't have any weird sexual habits.

"You're a bit slow on the uptake, Cindy, even though you work next to a medical clinic." He shook his head in mock disgust. "Ice packs," he repeated, "for all my ailments. I expect to have a lot of aches and pains tonight."

Smiling, she tilted her head provocatively. "Now I *know* you're a hypochondriac. I thought kisses cured all your ills."

"Dr. Marshall," he said, his grin positively lecherous, "you've got yourself a patient."

"But you said you were tired," she teased.

"I suddenly feel revived." He took her into her arms.

They didn't race to the bedroom; they didn't even run. And when they finally arrived, Brad discovered that he wasn't tired at all. And he didn't need ice packs, either. Cindy managed to soothe all his ailments with kisses, though later she swore he was the worst hypochondriac she'd ever encountered. He claimed that every inch of his body hurt.

"You'd think you were in an auto accident," she teased after they had made love again. He took her in his arms, complaining once more about his aching body. "If you're not careful, I'll put you in traction," she threatened.

"How about whips and chains instead?" he asked with feigned eagerness. "Hey! Want to try my handcuffs?"

"Brad!" she exclaimed, laughing.

"Ahh, Cindy." He pulled her into his arms. "You're too inhibited. You need to loosen up and enjoy life."

She snuggled against him. He wouldn't think so if he knew she'd strutted down a runway and taken off her clothes, not once, but hundreds of times. "How will handcuffs help me enjoy life?"

"I don't know, but if you're willing, I'll go first," he volunteered. "You can clip me to the bed and force me to do all sorts of things."

"I'll bet I wouldn't have to force you."

"You guessed it," he said. "I'm a moral degenerate."

"Too bad." She laughed, adding dryly, "Next, you'll suggest we make love in a jail cell."

"Nah, no fun," he said. "Have you ever seen a jail?"

At least now she could tell the truth easily. "Of course, I've seen a jail. Hasn't everyone?"

"I suppose, if you count television. Tired?" he asked when she yawned.

"A bit. Why?"

"I thought we might go out for ice cream."

"At this time of night?" The man suggested the strangest things at the weirdest times. "Brad, I'm beginning to think you can't sleep at night."

"You know, one of us is going to have to switch schedules. Ready to go out?"

"No, I'm not." They were both still naked and lying in bed. "I'm not dressed, and we'll never find ice cream at this time of night. Especially not rocky road ice cream."

"Sure we will," he said. "I'm not fussy. I like all kinds of ice cream. Any flavor will be fine."

Although she thought it was a crazy thing to do, Cindy got dressed and followed Brad out the door. "Will the cats be all right?" he asked as they left.

"They've been good this evening," Cindy said. At the moment they were curled up asleep on top of one another. "What about the police department? Will they be able to reach you if they need you?"

"They'll find me," he assured her, patting the small beeper in his pocket. "They always do. If necessary, the captain will call out the riot squad to track me down. We won't go far. There's a restaurant open right down the street."

Brad ate his ice cream as they walked back to her apartment. Cindy had decided not to have any. Though the hour was late, the night was balmy.

She strolled beside him, fascinated by the people on the streets. Saturday night in the city was busier than most evenings. Lovers strolled past, teenagers loitered on corners, and several men gathered in front of a nightclub. Down the block a movie house let out. On the street, cars and buses sped by.

Enjoying the walk, Cindy glanced idly in store windows. Brad pulled her close, his arm slung casually across her shoulders, his hand stroking absently up and down her arm.

"Want to have a look?" he asked as they approached a jewelry store. "I understand women like to window-shop."

"Unfortunately, we like to shop for real too," Cindy said, letting him lead her to the window display, where gems of all sizes and shapes glittered from black velvet—rings, necklaces, watches, and bracelets.

"Do you like diamonds? Wow!" He whistled under his breath. "Look at that one."

Pausing beside him, Cindy glanced at the glittering pear-shaped stone. "It's big enough to fit in my navel."

"How about your finger?"

She laughed. "That, too."

He pointed to a small gold, heart-shaped locket. "Nice locket."

"It looks like an antique," Cindy remarked.

Brad nodded. "I always wondered where people got pictures small enough to fit inside."

They stood still for a moment, lost in their own thoughts. Cindy rested her head on his shoulder as she stared at the locket and diamond. The ring was undeniably lovely.

"You know," Brad said softly, thoughtfully, a few moments later, "they say if you want to know what a woman is going to look like later in life, all you have to do is look at her mother."

"Who are *they?*" Cindy asked absently.

"The people who say those things. Statisticians? Psychologists?" He shrugged. "I don't know."

"I guess the theory could be true," she said, "but I would expect the father to have some influence, too."

"True." He kissed her gently on the forehead and pulled her closer, tucking her securely in his arms. "Who do you look like, Cindy? Your mother or your father?"

She hesitated only a moment. "My father."

"Do you have any pictures of him?"

"One. It's very old. I was just a kid. We were playing baseball together."

"How about your mother? Do you have a picture of her?"

"I have a couple of her, but they're old, too."

"You said you lived in Texas for a while. Were you alone then?"

"Yes. I ran away from home."

"How old were you?"

"Fourteen."

"That must have been tough. Have you seen your folks since then? Have you ever tried to contact them?"

To her surprise, she found that talking about her parents wasn't as difficult as she would have expected. "No, at first I didn't want to get caught and sent back. Then, as time drifted by, it became harder and harder to call. I never have."

"Were they cruel to you?"

"Sometimes. They were alcoholics."

He held her close in the long pause that followed. She waited in pained anticipation for what he would say next. Finally he whispered, "You need to make peace with them, Cindy."

It was the last thing she had expected him to say. His understanding and sympathy confused her. No lectures, no recriminations, no patronizing her, no further questions.

"I know," she whispered. She'd known it for a long time, but she'd put it off. Like other things. Like telling him about her past.

"I love you," he said.

She loved him, too. Oh, Lord, what was she going to do?

"It seems too fast, doesn't it? A few days?"

She couldn't speak; she was too choked up.

"They say it can happen that way," he went on softly, still stroking her hair.

"You know a lot of *theys*," she said, trying to be funny, trying very hard not to cry.

But her humor didn't succeed. Brad didn't laugh, and

neither did she, and she was already crying. Tears had welled up in her eyes. "Yes, I do," he agreed. "Cindy, don't cry."

But she couldn't help it. Tears streamed down her face.

Turning her toward him, Brad enfolded her in his arms, oblivious to people passing by. Cindy forgot they were on a busy street as he tenderly wiped the moisture from her eyes and bent to kiss her lips. "I can't stand it when you cry. It tears me apart."

"I'm sorry."

"Don't be. Cindy . . . say you love me."

She gazed at him through tear-filled eyes. *I love you, Brad,* she silently murmured. *I love you so very much.* But there was no joy in the unspoken declaration, only sorrow, for at that moment, she knew it was over between them. She had to tell him about her past, and she had to do it now, tonight. She couldn't put it off any longer.

And when she did tell him, she would lose him. She would never see him again, and she didn't know how she could bear that. Seeing the recrimination in his eyes would be even harder to bear. Yet she had no choice.

"Brad," she said softly, "we have to talk. There are some things I need to tell you."

"Cindy, honey—"

"Don't," she whispered, lowering her gaze to hide her distress. "Brad, please don't make it any harder than it already is. Can we just go home?"

"Okay." He stood silently for a long moment, then took her hand. "We'll talk. I want to know what's bothering you. Ready?"

"Yes," she lied. She'd never be ready, not for this. But she started to walk beside him. "I'm ready."

CHAPTER
Nine

As they returned to her apartment, Cindy was so nervous she could hardly speak. She ached so much inside, surely her heart was breaking.

The silence stretched interminably as they walked the few blocks from the jewelry store to her building, and up the steps. What was he thinking now? She didn't have any clues. He was quiet, his expression impassive.

Compounding her frustration, when she opened the door, she discovered that the kittens were awake now and back to their usual mischief. Sparky was sitting on a bookshelf, having knocked over the plant there. All the other kittens were crouched around the pile of dirt and leaves, playing with the broken vines. Sam lay on the sofa, calmly surveying the damage. What a big help she was!

"Darn it!" Cindy exclaimed. "Bad kitties!"

The sound of her voice sent the felines scattering in four directions.

"Why don't I put them in a closet?" Brad suggested. "Just for a few minutes, while we talk."

Cindy sighed. "Margie gave me laundry baskets. I think I'll use them until I can come up with something else." She put each cat under its own basket. To her surprise they seemed delighted with the new experience. Sparky crouched tigerlike, batting playfully at the plastic slats that enclosed him like the bars of a jail cell.

Cindy turned to Brad. How should she begin? She was anxious to get this over with—confessions weren't her strong point—but she kept thinking of Peter's face when she'd told him. "Do you want some coffee?"

"Coffee sounds good."

Grateful for something to do, she entered the kitchen and fussed at the stove. Brad followed.

"Cream and sugar?" Funny, after all they'd shared during the past few days, she still didn't know how he drank his coffee. They'd always had tea together.

"Just cream." Brad took off his jacket and hung it on the back of a chair, exposing the shoulder holster he always wore, the straps of which crisscrossed his back.

She went to the refrigerator. "I'm sorry, all I have is milk."

"Milk will be fine."

She set the milk carton on the table. This exchange of social chit-chat was silly. She had to force herself to stop procrastinating. She had to tell him.

She gestured to a chair. "Maybe you'd better... sit down."

Brad smiled. "Is it that bad?"

He was teasing her, trying to set her at ease, but Cindy didn't laugh. "Yes, it is that bad."

"Okay. I'm sitting."

She took a deep breath. There was no way to put it

off any longer. "Brad, do you remember when we first met, and I told you I didn't date?"

"Yes."

"Well, there are specific reasons why I don't date."

"We aren't dating, Cindy," he answered softly. "What we have is special. You know that."

Yes, they had something special, but she was obsessed with the idea that she'd deceived him. She'd fallen in love with him, and she'd let him fall in love with her, without being honest with him.

"Brad, I . . ." She would just have to blurt it out. Trying very hard not to cry, she opened her mouth to speak.

Brad reached across the table and took her hand in his. "Cindy, honey, you don't have to do this."

"Yes, I do," she insisted. "I have to tell you these things." She just had to get up the courage.

Suddenly the telephone rang. Saved by the bell, she thought. How convenient! She stood up quickly to answer. Damn! If it was Margie, she would strangle her friend.

But it was Wes, looking for Brad. She handed him the phone and stood to one side while he spoke briefly to the other detective. He'd been working on a case. Obviously the call was important.

"I'll be right there," he said in low tones. He hung up and turned to her. "Cindy, I'm sorry, but I have to go. That drug bust I told you about is going down now."

She nodded numbly. "I understand."

"Look, babe." He took her into his arms. Though she yearned for his strength, his warmth, she dared not let herself relax against him. "I know whatever it is you're trying to say is important to you, and I want to listen. I don't know how long this will take, but I'll be back as soon as I can, and we'll talk. Okay?" When she nodded again, he leaned down to brush his lips lightly across hers. "Come on. No more tears. If you keep crying, you're going to flood the city."

"I'm not crying."

"Good. Cindy, I wish I didn't have to leave."

"Brad, I understand," she said softly.

"Okay." With a heavy sigh he headed for the door, pulling on his jacket. When his sunglasses fell from his pocket, he paused. "Say, want to help me cross the street?"

He was teasing her again, trying to cheer her by reminding her of the day they'd met, but she felt as if her heart were being torn from her body. "I don't think I'd be much good tonight. I'd probably get you run over."

"You women are all alike," he joked. "Get a man's attention, make him need you, and then bingo! You won't even do him a simple favor." He kissed her again, briefly, his expression serious. "Cindy, don't worry, hon. Everything will be all right. We'll work it out together."

"Sure," she said softly.

"I'll be back," he repeated at the door. "Remember, Cindy, everything's going to be fine."

Standing in the doorway, she waited until Brad had clattered all the way down the steps and slammed the door of the building behind him. Then she pushed the apartment door softly shut, yet with a resounding finality.

He'd been so sincere, trying to reassure her, but she knew they could never work it out, because he didn't know yet what *it* was. Once he found out, he would reject her. That had been the pattern of her life, hadn't it? Every time she told a man about her past, he judged her harshly.

She sank down on the sofa, absently petting Sam, who was quietly grooming herself. Perhaps Brad would be different. Sure. What wishful thinking! She'd thought Peter was different, too.

Brad Jordan was one of the most upright, decent, moral men she'd ever met, and she knew deep down that he wouldn't be able to accept what she'd done earlier in her life. How could he? Although he lived in the city, he was a middle-class suburban man with middle-class suburban mores.

But he'd grown up in a tough Chicago neighborhood, hadn't he?

Behind her, Sparky meowed. Feeling guilty for caging the kittens, Cindy let them out from under the baskets and watched absently as they scampered around the room.

What bothered her most was that she hadn't been truthful and honest with Brad. She should have told him about her past the day they met. Earlier in the evening she'd told herself all she wanted was one night with him. She'd had that now. She shouldn't yearn for more.

Yet she did yearn for more, and all she could do was sit and wait for him to come back. Maybe she'd take a shower. Perhaps hot water streaming over her head would make her think more clearly. She headed for the bathroom.

The shower didn't help much. It hadn't done anything for her looks, either, she thought a few minutes later, staring into the bathroom mirror. She was a sight. Her eyes were red and swollen from her tears, and dark circles indicated her fatigue. Her towel-dried hair frizzed around her face. She grimaced at her reflection and went to the closet to find a pair of slacks and a blouse.

Cindy had almost finished dressing when, rummaging through a drawer, she found her pasties again. The gold threads sparkled up at her. One of these days she'd throw the stupid things away. For now she tossed them on top of the dresser, near an old photo cube.

Pausing for a moment, she glanced at the pictures. One showed Cindy and her father playing baseball; another was a close-up of her mother. She did look like her father; she had his blue eyes. She turned the cube. There was a picture of Sam, and another one of Sam and the kittens when they were little. The last picture was of Margie and Rebecca, which Cindy had taken outside of Club Arnaud years ago.

She stared at the photo of her friends for a long moment. They'd helped her so much. Rebecca had harassed her into going to college, and Margie, despite her brashness, had been there for her always, like a mother.

When her doorbell rang—Margie's special signal—Cindy was confused. It was well past one in the morning. What was Margie doing here now?

She didn't feel up to seeing her friend at the moment, but by then Margie was at the door and knocking. "Cindy!" she called excitedly. "Cindy, are you home?"

There was no sense hiding. She went to open the door. "Hi."

"Hi, yourself," Margie said, glancing at Cindy's attire. "What, no sexy nightgown tonight?"

"I was up."

Margie was wearing a hot pink jumpsuit that was conservative in comparison to her usual attire. "You look nice."

"Wish I could say the same for you," Margie countered. "You look awful. Every time I come here you look worse and worse."

"Thanks. You're just loaded with compliments tonight."

"You wouldn't want me to lie, would you?" Margie frowned as she pushed Sam off the sofa and sat down. "You been crying? Hey, kid, is something wrong?"

Cindy tried to smile. "What could be wrong?"

"I don't know, but you look really upset."

"I'm okay," Cindy answered. She wasn't upset; she was distraught, and trying very hard to maintain her composure. "Would you like some tea?"

"Boy, for someone who's feeling okay, you sure are acting weird. Cindy, I hate tea."

"Sorry, I forgot."

"Why don't you tell me what's bothering you, Cindy. You'll feel better if you talk it out, whatever it is."

What good would it do to confess to Margie how she felt? The redhead would just badger her. "Not tonight, Margie, but thanks."

"Have it your way," Margie said. "Just remember that I'll be willing to listen when you're ready to get things off your chest." With one foot she pushed away a kitten that had been rubbing against her leg. "Cindy, what the hell are you going to do with these damned cats? You're turning into the cat lady of Chicago."

Like the bird man of Alcatraz.

Prison.

Jail.

Cops.

Brad Jordan. Why did Margie have to bring up the subject? Cindy sighed. "They'll outgrow their mischievousness."

"That'll be the day." Margie grew serious. "Are you sure you won't tell me what's wrong?"

"Nothing's wrong."

"Yes, there is," Margie countered. "I know you, Cindy Marshall, and I can tell something's wrong. Do I have to drag it out of you? What the hell is it?"

Cindy glanced at her friend. "You should have been a lawyer, Margie."

"Why, because I talk so much?"

"No, because you never give up; you just keep hammering until you get an answer." Cindy sighed again and walked to the window to look outside. In the glow of the street lamps, the trees cast eerie shadows on the pavement below. "Remember those regrets we talked about the other night? Well, now I have even more of them."

"*You* should have been a *politician*," Margie said.

"You're getting really good at evading issues. Cindy, what's all this about?"

"I'm in love."

"With the blind guy?" Margie sounded delighted.

She nodded. "Unfortunately. Margie, I have to tell him about my past."

"Oh. And you're upset about that."

"Yes, I am."

"Don't forget, Cindy, you were just a kid when you got hooked on speed. And the stripping—well, what can I say? You had to eat. You had to survive."

"I know that." Margie had had to survive, too. In fact, because of their individual circumstances, all of the women who had worked at the club with Cindy had had survival uppermost in their minds. "I just know it'll come out sounding terribly sordid. How do you tell somebody 'I took uppers and downers. I took off my clothes. I strutted down a runway wearing a G-string and pasties. I wore a coin in my belly button and glued chains on my body'?"

"You just say it," Margie said. "What the hell, I pranced around in buckskin boots wielding a gold-studded six-shooter, and I was thirty-five years old. Bang. Bang."

Cindy smiled. When Margie talked about the past, it sounded more humorous than sordid. "By the way, did you come by for a reason?"

"Oh, yes!" Margie looked horrified. "But when I saw how upset you were, I forgot all about it."

"About what?"

"Club Arnaud. Oh, Cindy, I hate to tell you this right now, kid, but Club Arnaud's been raided. We're on television."

Cindy felt the blood drain from her face. "We're on television?" she whispered. "You and me?"

"Pictures of us. Do you remember those posters Tony kept in the hallway, his Hall of Fame? Well, I just saw

Naughty and Nice   161

them on the tube. I was watching a movie when they began interrupting it with news bulletins. I was going to call you, but then I figured, what the hell, if our pictures were going to be flashed all over the city, we might as well watch it together. Then when I got here, I saw how upset you were, and we started talking, and the Club Arnaud business slipped right out of my mind. Turn on the set and see for yourself."

"Oh, Lord," Cindy murmured. She flicked on the television set just as Wes Martin appeared on the screen. He was standing outside the nightclub, being interviewed by a reporter.

Several police cars, their blue lights flashing, were lined up in front of the club. Yellow barriers kept back a crowd of curiosity seekers who had gathered on the sidewalk.

"Yes, this has been one of our biggest drug busts this year," Wes was saying into the microphone. "We confiscated several pounds of pure cocaine."

"Club Arnaud is a Chicago institution," the reporter said. "Hasn't it been a source of drug traffic before now?"

"The club was clean until it changed ownership," Wes answered. "We got a tip earlier tonight about cocaine coming through here."

"Hey, he's kind of cute," Margie said, looking at Wes. "For a cop."

Cindy nodded, her attention focused on the television screen. If Brad's partner was there, so was Brad. Lord, what should she do? Had he known when he left her apartment that he was going to Club Arnaud?

As if on cue, Brad came out of the club and into the range of the cameras.

"He's cute too," Margie remarked.

"Detective Jordan," the reporter called out, "can you give us any other details regarding this case?"

"I don't know any more than what my partner has

already told you," Brad answered.

"What about the dancers?" the reported asked. "Were they arrested, too?"

"Yes," Brad said, "everyone has been detained for questioning."

"What are you doing now? Why are the police still inside?"

"We're looking for more narcotics," Brad said. "That's all I can tell you at the moment."

Turning away, he spoke quietly to Wes, and they both disappeared back inside. The reporter turned to the camera, waving his hand dramatically to indicate the scene. "Well, folks, there you have it from Detectives Jordan and Martin. Club Arnaud, one of Chicago's most popular nightclubs, was raided tonight. The police confiscated several pounds of cocaine, and they are currently searching the club for more narcotics."

Suddenly the camera swung around to the life-sized posters of the dancers as the reporter droned on and on, repeating the information Wes and Brad had given him, then filling time with general comments. "The club has long been attractive to out-of-town conventioneers," he said snidely.

"There I am," Margie squealed a few seconds later as the camera focused on her poster. "That's me! Hey, don't I look good? And that's you!"

Cindy wanted to close her eyes, but she couldn't. There, flashed on the television screen for the entire city to view, stood Freya, the Viking warrior maiden, in all her splendor. Cindy's long blond hair was interwoven with gold threads and piled high on her head, and a cape of gold chain mail fell regally from her shoulders. She looked like a warrior queen. More chain mail covered the essential parts of her body, and a coin was pasted in her navel. She smiled seductively—so naughty and yet so nice.

Abruptly she stood up and grabbed her purse. "I have to go."

Margie looked confused. "Go? Go where?"

"To talk to Brad." Cindy pulled open the door and ran down the stairs. "To tell him," she called.

"What about the cats?" Margie asked, slamming the door behind her. "Be good," she told them. "Brad who?"

"Brad Jordan."

"That guy on television, wasn't his name Jordan?" Margie asked as she clattered down the steps behind Cindy.

"Yes." Cindy ran out the front door to the corner, where someone was just getting out of a cab. As soon as the person disembarked she hopped in.

"Cindy, wait!" Margie said breathlessly as she piled into the cab behind her. "I don't understand. Where are we going?"

"I told you, to Club Arnaud. I have to tell him. I have to explain. Go," she told the driver, rattling off the address. "Now! I'm in a hurry."

The cabbie took her at her word, though she hardly noticed the wild, careening ride through the city streets. She was trying very hard not to fall apart. She kept clenching and unclenching her hands, staring straight ahead. *Why?* Why hadn't she told him sooner?

Only moments later, the cab screeched to a halt in front of the club. "Here you go, ma'am." Cindy paid the driver and got out.

Margie had been quiet during the cab ride, too. Now she grabbed Cindy's arm. "Hey kid, that blind man... is he a cop? Is he that cop on television? Are you dating a detective?"

"Yes."

"Holy Christmas!"

Cindy didn't bother to give her friend an explanation. She was more concerned about how to get to Brad. The reporters were still there, and the crowd jammed around the wooden barriers hadn't begun to disperse. A uniformed policeman guarded the entrance to the club. Cindy didn't know what she was going to do or how she was going to get past the officer. All she knew was that she had to see Brad. Now. Oh, Lord, he'd probably already seen the poster. She pushed through the crowd to the club entrance.

"Hold it, ma'am," the policeman said, reaching out to detain her. "Nobody's allowed inside."

"I have to see Detective Jordan," she said.

"Sorry, lady, no one's allowed inside."

"Please," she said, hating the way her voice quavered. "I have to see him now. Could you call him? I know he'll let me in."

"There's some of the dancers," someone in the crowd shouted. "Those two women. Their pictures were on television earlier." The man was carrying a small, battery-operated television set, and he'd apparently watched the bulletins as he stood outside the club.

"Ma'am?" the reporter said, shoving the microphone at Cindy. "Are you one of the dancers, ma'am?"

"No." She wasn't, not anymore. Growing frantic, Cindy turned back to the policeman. "Officer, please let me in."

The officer remained stoic. "Can't."

Just then, apparently overhearing the commotion, Brad came to the door. "Cindy!" He halted, staring at her in surprise. "What are you doing here?"

It was so good to seem him! "I came to talk to you, Brad. I have to tell you about... about—"

Obviously sensing a story, the reporter shoved the microphone in front of her again. "What do you have to tell Detective Jordan, ma'am?"

"Excuse us. This is a private conversation." Brad turned away from the newsman and pulled Cindy inside the nightclub.

"Hi, guys." Margie winked at both the guard and the reporter as she followed. "What's cookin'?"

Brad barely glanced at Margie. "Cindy, what are you doing here? I told you to wait at your place."

"I couldn't wait any longer. I had to tell you, Brad," she said quickly. Heedless of the police officers who had paused in the midst of their work to watch, she pulled him toward the hallway. "Look," she said, pointing to the large, colorful poster of herself. "That's me."

Brad frowned at her. "I know that."

"I—I was in my teens when I came here," she went on hurriedly, before she lost her nerve. Tears streamed slowly down her face. "I was hooked on speed, and I stripped. I—I took off my clothes. Later, I went through a drug rehabilitation program, and—"

"Cindy," he cut in softly. "Babe, you don't have to tell me this."

"Yes, I do. You have to know. I didn't quit stripping until I was twenty-five years old."

"I already know all those things, Cindy."

"I straightened my life up, Brad," she went on. "I put myself through college and got a good job, but I have a past, and I can't deny it. I can't hide it from you." Suddenly his words registered in her mind, and she paused to stare up at him. "You *know?*" she whispered. "Are you saying you know—you *knew* about me and my past all along?"

"I didn't know *you*, Cindy Marshall, the person. Not until we started dating. But I did find out about your past right after I met you. You have a record. You were arrested several times. It all showed up on the computer."

"You punched up my police record on the computer?" she said unbelievingly. *"Why?"*

"How else was I supposed to find you in a city this size?" Brad asked. "I tried the phone company first, of course, but they wouldn't give me your unlisted number, so I ran your name through the computer on the chance that it would help me find you, and it did."

"Did you know right away, when you met me, that I had a record? Why else would you look it up in the computer?"

"Of course I didn't know right away, Cindy. I simply wanted to find you. I thought maybe we'd have a car license registered to you. Or you could have been on file as a victim or a witness or for any of a dozen other reasons. It was just by dumb luck that I happened on your arrest record."

"Oh," she said. Everything imaginable could be stored on tiny microchips the size of pin heads—biorhythms, horoscopes, pet pedigrees, police records...

"Did you think your past would matter to me?" he asked.

"Yes."

"It doesn't."

"Oh, Brad," she murmured. "Why didn't you tell me?"

"Because it didn't make any difference to me." He tenderly wiped the tears from her eyes and swept a lock of hair back from her face. "Cindy, I thought you knew that. I had a rough childhood, too. I told you I stole car parts."

"But tonight—"

"Tonight I didn't know what you wanted to tell me. I thought it had something to do with your parents. Cindy, I'm sorry if I've hurt you or made things harder for you. I thought you trusted me. I wanted you to trust me enough to tell me about your family."

"I—I thought you would be shocked. After all, you're a policeman."

"Maybe that's why I'm not shocked. I'll admit, at first I was surprised by your past. But then I got to know you. It's what you are now that counts, Cindy," he said softly, "not what you did years ago."

She stood for a moment savoring his words. "Oh, Brad."

"Come here, babe," he said. She went into his arms, resting her head against his chest. "Just for the record, your past doesn't and will never matter to me."

"I was so afraid." Her words were muffled against his chest.

"Don't ever be afraid, Cindy. Not with me. I love you."

"And I love you, she murmured. "Oh, how I love you."

CHAPTER
Ten

BRAD HELD CINDY in his arms for a long moment, comforting her. He tipped her chin up. "Come on. Let's go home."

"You can just leave?"

"I was almost finished when you arrived. Wes will handle the paperwork."

Just now realizing that Wes was standing beside them, grinning from ear to ear, Cindy managed to smile at him. "Oh!" she said, suddenly remembering her friend. "Margie! I can't leave her here."

"I can manage, kid," Margie said from behind her. "But don't you think it's about time I met your friend? Even if he is the fuzz," she added, holding out her hand.

"Good to meet you, Margie," Brad said, shaking her hand. He indicated Wes. "My partner, Wes Martin."

Margie turned to the older detective and tilted her

head provocatively. "How are you getting home, big boy?"

"Driving," Wes answered, his grin broadening. "Need a lift?"

Cindy was amazed at how brazenly Margie was flirting with Wes, smiling and batting her eyelashes. "You driving a squad car?"

"I can, if that's what you want to ride in."

"Sweetie, I've probably ridden in more squad cars than you have." She took his arm. "But I've never ridden in the front seat."

Wes laughed. "One front seat coming up."

Without a backward glance, Margie allowed herself to be escorted away. Cindy stared after her. "Did you see my picture up there?" Margie was saying to Wes as they exited through the front door. "That's me in the buckskin boots."

Brad laughed when they had disappeared from sight. "I think Wes has met his match. Does she know how to cook?"

"Margie?" Cindy shook her head. "No."

"Oh, well." Brad slung an arm across her shoulders. "Come on. Let's get out of here."

They had walked only a short distance when Margie hurried back into the darkened club. "Cindy," she hissed, crooking her finger. "Come here."

Puzzled, Cindy extracted herself from Brad's embrace and walked to where Margie was standing. "Yes?"

"What do cops do at a ball?"

"Dance."

"For real dance, or that slow, stodgy crap?"

"I think a combination of both."

"Oh, good. Hey, if I stop by tomorrow will you give me the recipe for apple spice pie?" Margie asked. "Wes just told me he likes home cooking." Then, excitedly, "Did you ever think I'd go out with the fuzz?"

"No," Cindy said, shaking her head, "I never did." But then, she'd never have believed *she'd* go out with "the fuzz" either.

Margie winked. "Hey, I gotta go. Wes is waiting for me out front. What about that recipe?"

"You're going to bake a pie?"

"No, I'm going to buy it," Margie said sarcastically. "You know, you've really gotten to be a smart-ass these days. Of course, I'm going to bake it."

"Sorry. Sure, stop by anytime."

Margie grinned. "Thanks. See you, huh?"

"Right." Cindy watched as Margie left the club, swinging her purse and her hips.

"What was that all about?" Brad asked, coming up beside her.

"Never mind. You wouldn't believe it anyhow. Does Wes like apple spice pie?"

"Wes likes any pie."

"Good. I only hope he likes it burned."

They started toward the door. Even though she'd confessed her past to Brad, Cindy was reluctant to go outside and face the television cameras. She had a feeling she was going to be more notorious now than she had been as Freya, the Viking maiden, and she wasn't certain she was up to it.

At the entrance she hesitated, but Brad squeezed her shoulder reassuringly, as though guessing her thoughts. "Don't worry. It'll be fine. I'll get you out."

True to his word, he firmly waved away the reporters. "The party's over, boys. Stay tuned. The captain will issue an official statement in the morning."

He hurried her down the street toward his car. Cindy was getting inside when a tall man broke away from a group of people walking by. "Say," he said to Cindy, "don't I know you from somewhere?"

Brad stiffened. "Look, buddy—"

"It's okay." Cindy touched his arm as she turned to the stranger. If someone had come up to her yesterday and made that kind of remark, she would have been upset and angry. Now she didn't mind. Brad had made the difference. "Did you ever sell pickles?" she asked the man. "I used to work at Club Arnaud."

"Pickles?" The stranger frowned in confusion as Brad squeezed her hand approvingly. "No, I never sold pickles," the man said. "I remember now. I met you at the Crisis Center. You're the social worker who's counseling my brother's daughter. Her name's Nicole. Nicole Rogers."

Now Cindy recognized him, too. The Rogers family was close-knit. Several of them had been at the center, giving their brother moral support on the day Nicole had arrived at the clinic. "Oh, yes, I remember."

Nicole and her father just had a great weekend together," the man went on. "For the first time in years they've been able to talk, thanks to you," he added, shaking his head. "Imagine that. Meeting you here on the street in downtown Chicago. Small world, huh?"

Cindy was glad things were going well with Nicole. She'd been so wrapped up in her own problems this weekend that she'd almost forgotten the teens she counseled. "Yes," she said. "It is a small world."

"Well, thanks for helping my niece," the man said, starting to leave. Abruptly he turned back to her. "By the way, what did you do at Club Arnaud? It's right down the block, isn't it?"

Brad put an arm around her waist. "She used to dance there."

"No kidding? Is that how you put yourself through college?"

"Yes," she said.

"Good for you. An education's important." The man smiled again and waved. "See you sometime."

When Brad closed the car door and got in on his side, Cindy turned to him. "Thanks."

"For what?"

"For supporting me."

He smiled and drew her close. "Have I told you lately that I love you?"

"Yes," she murmured.

"No," he said, holding her tightly. "I mean, I *love* you . . . forever."

Tears sprang to Cindy's eyes, tears of joy. "Brad—"

"We're wasting time," he said.

"What do you mean?"

"Cindy, you talk too much."

She talked too much! She laughed. "Tell me, Lieutenant Jordan, is there something else you want to do instead of talk?"

"Yes," he murmured huskily. "Didn't you say cats sleep during the day?"

What did that have to do with anything? She paused cautiously. "Yes, they do."

"Well, it's almost daylight. Just think, once the sun comes up, we won't have to close the bedroom door."

She laughed again, but the teasing lights in her eyes faded as he took her into his arms and kissed her in the darkened interior of the Porsche.

"Damned gearshift," he said a few moments later, sighing raggedly. "Look, Cindy, when we buy our station wagon, remind me to get an automatic transmission."

"Don't you like the gearshift between us?"

"Babe, I don't like anything between us."

When they got to her apartment, Brad ignored the kittens and the mess they'd made. He ignored her protest as well—that she had to clean up the stuffing from her sofa cushions—and purposefully undoing her buttons, backing her into the bedroom. "No more talk, Cindy," he said. "Just action."

He made love to her slowly, tenderly, touching her gently, as though she were a fragile flower requiring exquisite care. At the height of their passion he murmured, "Cindy, I love you."

"I love you, too, Brad," she whispered back. Their lovemaking transcended anything she'd ever known. The universe spun away. Stars exploded and crashed around her. Suns and moons sparkled with intense light. The white picket fence and the spacious house she dreamed about flitted into her consciousness, and a golden glow of fulfillment flooded through the core of her being.

Later, she snuggled next to him. She felt so special, so fortunate. Men like Brad Jordan were very rare. She traced a pattern across his chest with a fingernail. "Brad, can we talk now?"

"Hmmm?" he murmured, nuzzling her hair with his lips. "Sure. What do you want to talk about?"

"Lots of things."

He shifted so that they faced each other. "Okay, shoot. Subject one."

"First of all, did you know you were going to raid Club Arnaud tonight?"

"No, not till I met Wes. Second question?"

"That day you came to the Crisis Center. Did you really come just to see me?"

"Yes."

"Why?"

"You intrigued me. No woman had ever run away from me before. You're pretty, too."

She had a feeling he wasn't telling her the whole truth, but she gladly accepted his flattery. "What about that night we went to the beach and ended up going for a carriage ride? Did you plan that?"

"No. But when we went past Club Arnaud, I realized you were upset, and that you had some emotional scars."

"You didn't pressure me for answers."

"I wanted you to trust me, Cindy. And at that point I wasn't certain how we felt about each other. I thought we might have something pretty special going, but I wasn't sure I was ready to make a commitment to anyone. Now I feel differently about that. And speaking of commitments, do you think you can get a few days off?"

The tenderness in his voice told her he wanted to spend those days with her. "Yes, I have vacation time coming up. Why?"

"So we can get married."

"Oh."

Brad leaned over her on one elbow. *"Oh?* I ask you to marry me and that's all you can say?"

She smiled. "I thought you didn't want any attachments," she teased.

"No attachments to fake birds, but I'm in the mood for a few cats. Cindy, maybe after you get the kittens trained, we should buy a condominium here in the city. What do you think?"

"Only if we don't use your decorator."

"I thought you liked satin sheets."

"You thought of the sheets," she said. *"She* thought of that poster in your kitchen."

"The orange? Don't you like it?"

"It's awful. Besides, who knows if I'll ever get the kittens trained?"

"I have faith."

Cindy smiled, but at his soft words, she had started to cry again. Her tears of joy were becoming as frequent as her tears of sadness had once been.

"Babe? What's the matter?"

"Oh, Brad."

He held and kissed her. "Don't cry, Cindy."

"I'm not crying."

"What's that water running down your face?"

"I'm happy."

"Oh, okay." He laughed and hugged her close. "Hey!" he said suddenly. "I'm hungry. Let's go out and get some egg rolls."

"Brad, it's the middle of the night."

"I suppose you're tired. I told you you were going to have to switch hours, Cindy Marshall."

"Me? What about you?"

"I'm a great detective."

"Sure, sure, I know all about that, but even great detectives can work days."

"I like working nights," he said. "I get to flirt with pretty ladies."

"And take them to the beach," she said, "and on carriage rides."

"And marry them," he agreed. A few minutes later, he said softly, "You know something, Cindy? You're beautiful. Inside, outside, upside down, or sideways, you're the most beautiful woman I've ever known."

Though touched by his words, she couldn't help teasing him. "Because I don't mind going sunbathing at three A.M.?"

He laughed again. "No, because you're you."

"Thank you," she whispered, thinking it was odd how things had worked out. Instead of gathering a few rose petals, she'd accumulated an entire bouquet. She had a man who loved her, with a forever kind of love, and they were going to get married. It was too good to be true.

They should have closed the bedroom door. When something fell from her dresser with a metallic clink, Cindy glanced over. Sparky was stepping dauntily among the bottles. Of all the cats, he was the most curious. "Scat!" she said.

"I'll get him." Brad slipped out of bed, and flipped on a light, then grabbed the cat and put it on the floor. Then he paused and picked up her photo cube, glancing at the pictures. "You do look like your father," he said. "Very much."

Cindy nodded. She hesitated for a moment, then said quietly, "I've decided to call Boston later."

As Brad turned to her, she read approval in his eyes. "It's been a long time. Do you think you can find them?"

"I can try. I'm ready now. Who knows, maybe I can help them. After all, I'm a social worker. I just hope it's not too late."

"It won't be," he assured her. He was being optimistic, and they both knew it, but she appreciated his encouragement.

"Will you help me?"

"I'll be there." He discovered her pasties and held them up interestedly. "What are these?"

Damn! She'd forgotten all about them. She'd better throw the things away. "I think you know what they are."

He shook his head with feigned innocence. "Not me."

"Brad."

He grinned. "I wish I could have seen you up on that stage, Cindy. I'll bet you were good."

"Listen, buddy," she said, standing and wrapping the sheet around her body. She took the pasties from his hand and held them up, letting them dangle so that they caught the light. "I used to be able to twirl these things in different directions."

"I'll bet that was a splendid sight. You wouldn't consider showing me, would you?"

She pretended to contemplate his request. "Maybe. Do you have any pickles?"

He laughed again and took her into his arms. "Cindy," he murmured in her ear, "I've been meaning to tell you, I've got this pain."

"Brad!" She bashed him over the head with the pillow. "Stop!"

"But it really hurts."

"Sure." She tossed the pasties onto the dresser. Sparky jumped up and grabbed one, intrigued by the sparkle, but Cindy ignored the cat. Who cared about a pair of pasties?

She started to unwrap the sheet from her body. "Come here, Mr. Jordan. I have just the cure for what ails you."

COMING NEXT MONTH

TANGLING WITH WEBB #346 by Laine Allen
Writer's block drives whimsical Cristy McKnight
to a rash wager with wickedly handsome, infuriatingly
smug Webster Cannon: She'll concoct his
mystery if he'll pen her romance!

FRENCHMAN'S KISS #347 by Kerry Price
So what if he makes beautiful music, cooks
divinely, and kisses exquisitely? Thoroughly
unpredictable French composer Jean-Claude Delacroix
is *not* the reliable companion Sherry Seaton requires.

KID AT HEART #348 by Aimée Duvall
Where toy designer Lisa Fleming goes,
chaos follows—to the chagrin...and delight...
of toy company owner Chase Sanger, who begins
to hope he's found a lifelong playmate!

MY WILD IRISH ROGUE #349 by Helen Carter
Darkly handsome, joyfully spontaneous,
Liam Claire teases and tempts reserved Ingrid Peterson,
pursuing her across Ireland until she's nervous,
confused...and *very* aroused!

HAPPILY EVER AFTER #350 by Carole Buck
Lily Bancroft will do anything to get
the money—even dress as Snow White—but nothing
on earth will ever turn ruthlessly powerful
Dylan Chase into a fairy-tale prince.

TENDER TREASON #351 by Karen Keast
Wealthy, elusive, dictatorial Nyles Ryland electrifies
insurance investigator Lauren Kane with silken caresses
and drugging kisses. But she has no intention of playing
this week's lover to Grand Cayman's mystery man...

Be Sure to Read These New Releases!

SWANN'S SONG #334 by Carole Buck
Knowing both karate and kids, Megan Harper poses
as a nanny to secretly guard rock star Colin Swann and
his irrepressible son...and gets into deep
trouble when love complicates the deception!

STOLEN KISSES #335 by Liz Grady
Mattie Hamilton is rehearsing a museum
heist when tuxedo-clad thief Devlin Seamus Devlin
tackles her in midair...and offers to tutor
her in *all* kinds of midnight maneuvers!

GOLDEN GIRL #336 by Jacqueline Topaz
In sophisticated Hollywood, schoolteacher Olivia Gold
finds both her movie star grandmother *and* dashing soulmate
Andrew Carr—who transforms her into a glittering
golden girl and spellbinds her with sensual enchantment.

SMILES OF A SUMMER NIGHT #337 by Delaney Devers
Like a modern rogue, plantation owner
Jules Robichaux sweeps April Jasper away with cynical
charm, smoothly seduces her under moonlit
magnolias...but won't trust her enough to offer his love.

DESTINY'S DARLING #338 by Adrienne Edwards
"Bought" by ex-husband Bart Easton at a charity
benefit, Dot Biancardi recalls poignant moments—of
gallant courtship, wedded bliss...and lonely
heartache. Dare she risk repeating past mistakes?

WILD AND WONDERFUL #339 by Lee Williams
Trapped on a wild Maine island with brawny recluse
Greg Bowles, who's rejected the inheritance she's come to
give him, heir hunter Alicia Saunders finds a new
tension building...desire quickening.

Order on opposite page

___ 0-425-08750-6	SWEETS TO THE SWEET #311 Jeanne Grant	$2.25
___ 0-425-08751-4	EVER SINCE EVE #312 Kasey Adams	$2.25
___ 0-425-08752-2	BLITHE SPIRIT #313 Mary Haskell	$2.25
___ 0-425-08753-0	MAN AROUND THE HOUSE #314 Joan Darling	$2.25
___ 0-425-08754-9	DRIVEN TO DISTRACTION #315 Jamisan Whitney	$2.25
___ 0-425-08850-2	DARK LIGHTNING #316 Karen Keast	$2.25
___ 0-425-08851-0	MR. OCTOBER #317 Carole Buck	$2.25
___ 0-425-08852-9	ONE STEP TO PARADISE #318 Jasmine Craig	$2.25
___ 0-425-08853-7	TEMPTING PATIENCE #319 Christina Dair	$2.25
___ 0-425-08854-5	ALMOST LIKE BEING IN LOVE #320 Betsy Osborne	$2.25
___ 0-425-08855-3	ON CLOUD NINE #321 Jean Kent	$2.25
___ 0-425-08908-8	BELONGING TO TAYLOR #322 Kay Robbins	$2.25
___ 0-425-08909-6	ANYWHERE AND ALWAYS #323 Lee Williams	$2.25
___ 0-425-08910-X	FORTUNE'S CHOICE #324 Elissa Curry	$2.25
___ 0-425-08911-8	LADY ON THE LINE #325 Cait Logan	$2.25
___ 0-425-08948-7	A KISS AWAY #326 Sherryl Woods	$2.25
___ 0-425-08949-5	PLAY IT AGAIN, SAM #327 Petra Diamond	$2.25
___ 0-425-08966-5	SNOWFLAME #328 Christa Merlin	$2.25
___ 0-425-08967-3	BRINGING UP BABY #329 Diana Morgan	$2.25
___ 0-425-08968-1	DILLON'S PROMISE #330 Cinda Richards	$2.25
___ 0-425-08969-X	BE MINE, VALENTINE #331 Hilary Cole	$2.25
___ 0-425-08970-3	SOUTHERN COMFORT #332 Kit Windham	$2.25
___ 0-425-08971-1	NO PLACE FOR A LADY #333 Cassie Miles	$2.25
___ 0-425-09117-1	SWANN'S SONG #334 Carole Buck	$2.25
___ 0-425-09118-X	STOLEN KISSES #335 Liz Grady	$2.25
___ 0-425-09119-8	GOLDEN GIRL #336 Jacqueline Topaz	$2.25
___ 0-425-09120-1	SMILES OF A SUMMER NIGHT #337 Delaney Devers	$2.25
___ 0-425-09121-X	DESTINY'S DARLING #338 Adrienne Edwards	$2.25
___ 0-425-09122-8	WILD AND WONDERFUL #339 Lee Williams	$2.25
___ 0-425-09157-0	NO MORE MR. NICE GUY #340 Jeanne Grant	$2.25
___ 0-425-09158-9	A PLACE IN THE SUN #341 Katherine Granger	$2.25
___ 0-425-09159-7	A PRINCE AMONG MEN #342 Sherryl Woods	$2.25
___ 0-425-09160-0	NAUGHTY AND NICE #343 Jan Mathews	$2.25
___ 0-425-09161-9	ALL THE RIGHT MOVES #344 Linda Raye	$2.25
___ 0-425-09162-7	BLUE SKIES, GOLDEN DREAMS #345 Kelly Adams	$2.25

Available at your local bookstore or return this form to:

SECOND CHANCE AT LOVE
THE BERKLEY PUBLISHING GROUP, Dept. B
390 Murray Hill Parkway, East Rutherford, NJ 07073

Please send me the titles checked above. I enclose _____. Include $1.00 for postage and handling if one book is ordered; 25¢ per book for two or more not to exceed $1.75. New York residents please add sales tax. Prices are subject to change without notice and may be higher in Canada.

NAME_____

ADDRESS_____

CITY_____ STATE/ZIP_____

(Allow six weeks for delivery.) SK-41b

A STIRRING PAGEANTRY OF *HISTORICAL ROMANCE*

Shana Carrol
___ 0-515-08249-X Rebels in Love $3.95

Roberta Gellis
___ 0-515-07529-9 Fire Song $3.95
___ 0-515-08600-2 A Tapestry of Dreams $3.95

Jill Gregory
___ 0-515-07100-5 The Wayward Heart $3.50
___ 0-515-08710-6 My True and Tender Love $3.95
___ 0-515-08585-5 Moonlit Obsession $6.95
(A Jove Trade Paperback)
___ 0-515-08389-5 Promise Me The Dawn $3.95

Mary Pershall
___ 0-425-09171-6 A Shield of Roses $3.95
___ 0-425-09079-5 A Triumph of Roses $3.95

Francine Rivers
___ 0-515-08181-7 Sycamore Hill $3.50
___ 0-515-06823-3 This Golden Valley $3.50

Pamela Belle
___ 0-425-08268-7 The Moon in the Water $3.95
___ 0-425-07367-X The Chains of Fate $6.95
(A Berkley Trade Paperback)

Shannon Drake
___ 0-515-08637-1 Blue Heaven, Black Night $7.50
(A Jove Trade Paperback)

Available at your local bookstore or return this form to:

BERKLEY
THE BERKLEY PUBLISHING GROUP, Dept. B
390 Murray Hill Parkway, East Rutherford, NJ 07073

Please send me the titles checked above. I enclose _____. Include $1.00 for postage and handling if one book is ordered; 25¢ per book for two or more not to exceed $1.75. California, Illinois, New Jersey and Tennessee residents please add sales tax. Prices subject to change without notice and may be higher in Canada.

NAME_____
ADDRESS_____
CITY_____ STATE/ZIP_____

(Allow six weeks for delivery.)